D1711972

Other
Sammy and Brian Mysteries
by Ken Munro

The Quilted Message
The Bird in the Hand
Amish Justice
Jonathan's Journal
Doom Buggy
Fright Train
Creep Frog
The Number Game
The Tin Box
The Toy Factory
The Medallion's Secret
Secret Under the Floorboard
The Mysterious Guest House
Fire, Smoke, and Secrets
Fireball
Grandfather's Secret
The Mysterious Baseball Scorecard
The Cross Keys Caper
The Buggy Heist
The Indian Bones' Revenge

The Sammy and Brian Mysteries are available at special quantity discounts for sales promotion, fund-raisers, or educational uses. For details, write to:

Gaslight Publishers
1916 Barton Drive
Lancaster, PA 17603

Email: kemunro@comcast.net

BLUE DOG

A SAMMY & BRIAN MYSTERY #21

BY KEN MUNRO

GASLIGHT PUBLISHERS

Blue Dog

Copyright © 2010
by Ken Munro

Illustration by: Dick Weidman

Gaslight Publishers
1916 Barton Drive
Lancaster, PA 17603

Email: kemunro@comcast.net
sammyandbrianmysteries.com

Library of Congress Number: 2010926425
International Standard Book Number: 978-1-60126-227-1

Printed 2010 at
Masthof Press
219 Mill Road
Morgantown, PA 19543-9516

DEDICATION

To all my fans who
insist I write "just one more."
Well, here it is,
another "just one more."

Special thanks to:

Cathy Trissel
Ron Munro
Gene Hansen
Tracy Palmer

CHAPTER ONE

His head labored to the right as his listless eyes scanned each person in the room. The sickness dulled his vision. His eyes squinted and rested on one ghostlike image. Yes, *that's* the one, he thought. He wasn't so far gone that he couldn't recognize the person who plagued his dreams for the last 15 years.

Now, he had nothing to lose. In a couple of hours he would be dead.

The ever-spreading sickness left him weak, his strength gone. He could hardly speak. He made a final motion toward the phone, twisting his body and stretching his arm and fingers. But the phone remained an inch beyond his reach.

Everyone in the room gasped as John Mason made his unexpected show of desperation. The moment intensified as the nurse adjusted his hospital bed.

"He's not strong enough to make any phone

calls," came a voice from the relatives and visitors who filled the hospital room.

It was too late. With determination, John rolled over, grasped the phone, and carefully dialed. His wife moved forward, but the husband's bony hand warded her off.

The room was still as the old man touched the phone to his lips. The persistent ringing slowly drained any hope from his face. However, a slight flicker of life returned when the phone offered to record a message.

The patient's free hand cupped his mouth. His voice lowered as he started the frail words that would bring him final peace. "Sammy Wilson, this is John Mason."

CHAPTER TWO

Brian's wet face pressed against the glass as he rang the doorbell. He saw Sammy's mother look up from the kitchen table. The unexpected rainfall caught the amateur detective unprepared. He didn't care much about his bike getting wet, but he hated rain on his head. Water turned his wavy hair into ringlets. Brian rarely wore a head covering because he didn't want to mess up his hair. If his head did get wet, he would apply a cap to persuade his hair to dry straight.

Sammy Wilson and Brian Helm were fifteen-year-old amateur detectives who lived in Bird-in-Hand and solved mysteries in Lancaster County. Sammy was the brighter of the two, often referred to as a young Sherlock Holmes. Brian, on the other hand, lived in his own private world of secret agents and escapism. At times, he fancied himself as Double-Oh-Seven-and-a-Half, which gave him license to brag. Humor helped him ease negative situations.

The pathetic face at the door motivated Mrs. Wilson to rush to Brian's aid. "Oh, you boys think you're too macho to wear a raincoat or to carry an umbrella," she said, allowing Brian to slip by her into the kitchen.

Brian winced at the scolding, realizing that mothers have to say things like that. He visualized a book of sayings that had to be read and memorized by would-be mothers. How else could you account for all mothers making the same speeches?

"It wasn't supposed to rain today," he said. "We had enough rain yesterday." He raised his T-shirt to his head and blotted his hair. "Is Sammy here?" he said.

"Sammy's father drove him out to the Glicks' farm. He got a call from Detective Phillips. Something about furniture being stolen from several Amish farms. Do you know about it?"

Brian's eyes opened wide. "No."

"He said, if you called or came by, I was to tell you to meet him there."

Brian felt his hair. "Hey, does Sammy have a baseball cap I can borrow to flatten my hair?"

Mrs. Wilson shook her head as she headed for the living room. She had tried countless times to persuade Brian to allow his hair to curl. He always replied the same way, "Curly hair makes you look like a sissy."

"Here, I found these in the closet," Mrs. Wilson said when she returned. She held a baseball cap and a rain jacket. A Sammy Wilson name tag was stitched on the upper pocket area.

Brian squeezed the cap onto his head and sneered at the jacket.

Sammy's mother held the coat open for Brian. "If you're going to ride your bike out to the farm in this rain, you'll need this. It will keep you dry."

Brian checked the weather through the window. It was still raining, so he slipped his arms into the sleeves and adjusted the coat around his shoulders. He raised a sleeve to his nose and sniffed. "It smells musty."

"Sammy wore this yesterday during the storm. It's still a little damp. I told him to let it dry in the bathroom, but you know kids. They don't listen to their mothers." Mrs. Wilson checked her watch. "I'd run you out to the farm in my car, but I have to tend the store. I'm here alone, except for my part-time help."

Sammy's parents ran the Bird-in-Hand Country Store in a building next to their house. They sold Amish quilts, wall hangings, and other Amish-made crafts.

Brian stood tall with his shoulders back. He took a deep breath and faced the door. In his deepest voice, he announced, "That's okay, Mrs. Wilson. We who put our lives on the line everyday face the unknown, regardless of the dangers. We go forth, sacrificing our lives so that others may live secure from the evildoers and other scum who infect our lives."

Mrs. Wilson held the door open for Brian. "In the meantime," she said, "I'll call your mommy and tell her to have a large bowl of hot soup ready for you when you get home." She reached for a dishtowel. "Here, dry your bike seat. It wouldn't look right to have our heroes parading around in wet pants."

CHAPTER THREE

The black car pulled into the last parking space in front of the Bird-in-Hand Country Store. Rain marred the expectation that any tourist might have of seeing the Amish pushing their scooters along Main Street. Instead, tourists were running around, in and out of shops, trying to dodge raindrops. However, the driver in the black car sat quietly. The bucket hat he wore had a wide, downwards-sloping brim. Sunglasses and the mustache on his half-hidden face added mystery to the new arrival. He was in no hurry. His plan was to observe, identify, and then take appropriate action.

He twitched as he saw the teenager, wearing a cap and a jacket, leaving the house. He smiled as the boy failed in his attempt to dry his bicycle seat with a cloth. When the cloth became wetter than the seat, the man lowered the car window.

Brian glanced up through the rain and shrugged at the man watching him. "I think I'll go back inside and wait for the rain to stop," he yelled.

The man waved. "Hey, come over here. I was waiting for the rain to quit before I came to the house." He extended his hand out the window. "I'm Carl Rutter. I'd like to write a book about you and your partner."

Brian forgot about the rain as he stood tall and entered his secret agent mode. Helm, Brian Helm, Double-Oh-Seven and a Half, had images of book signings and public appearances. *Finally,* he thought, *my crime-fighting experiences will be revealed to the world.* He moved to the car, smiled, and shook the man's hand.

The man withdrew his arm from the window and started the car. "I bet you're hungry. Get in. I'll buy you lunch, and we can talk."

The window closed before Brian could answer.

Mrs. Wilson, watching from the kitchen window, didn't like the idea of Brian getting into a car with a stranger. *Maybe the man offered to drive Brian to the farm,* she thought. *Or maybe . . .*

The car backed out and headed east on Main Street. Mrs. Wilson attempted to record the license number, but the rain made it impossible.

*****

The Bird-in-Hand Farmer's Market sat back from Main Street, providing ample parking in front. The same was not true of the stools at Brenda's Snack Counter inside. Seating was limited, and while it wasn't the Ritz, it was enough for a writer to extract information from a fifteen-year-old boy.

"Well, hello, *Sammy*," Brenda said in a teasing tone. She was a small woman in her forties with short blond hair.

Brian shook off the beads of raindrops and draped his jacket over the stool. He looked up and said, "What?"

Brenda pointed and winked. "Your coat. It has your name on it, *Sammy*."

"Oh, yeah. Ha, ha." Brian said. He couldn't resist and added, "Well, hello, *Brenda's Snack Counter*." He pointed at the wall. "That sign has your name on it."

Carl Rutter, still wearing his hat and sunglasses, said abruptly, "I'll have a burger with mustard and onions and coffee. What do you want, Sammy?"

For the first time, Brian realized that Carl Rutter believed that he was Sammy Wilson. A tingling sensation traveled through Brian's body. He could agree to that, and besides, he often thought of himself as Sammy. He could play the part easily. He'd show this writer just how smart he was. This could be a chapter in the book: How Brian Helm became Sammy Wilson for a day.

"Well, 'Sammy,' what do you want?" Brenda said.

Brian glanced at the writer, who had a pen and pad in his hand. The teenager raised himself up, looked at Brenda, and said strongly, "I'll have my usual, a hotdog with sauerkraut on the side and a glass of milk."

"Milk?" Carl said, almost laughing.

"Milk? Did I say milk?" Brian said. "I meant a . . . a hefty mug of root beer."

Brenda raised her eyebrows and backed away to fill the order.

Brian looked at Carl Rutter and waited.

The writer, feeling uneasy, shrugged. "What?" he said.

Brian pointed to the notepad. "Aren't you going to write that down?"

"Write what down?" Carl said, frowning.

Brian thought for a moment, then answered, "Write down that the super sleuth ordered a hotdog with sauerkraut on the side. It provides brainpower for the super complex thinking necessary for fighting crime. Did I tell you that Brian Helm also eats hotdogs with sauerkraut on the side?"

Carl shook his head in disbelief. He adjusted his thinking to plan B: take away the carrot on the stick. "This is just the preliminary interview to see if your amateur detective adventures warrant a book," he said. "It could end up as a magazine article, or nothing at all."

The gloom and disappointment Brian felt lasted halfway though his lunch. Then Carl got Brian's attention. He sipped at his coffee and started writing on his notepad. "I bet you're working on an important case right now," he said.

"Oh, yes, Brian and I are investigating--" Brian stopped. No way was this going to be a magazine article. This was big book stuff, so to impress the writer, he said, "Sorry, but I can't reveal the details. It's so big that we can't talk about it. It's privileged information between amateur detectives and their client."

Carl's eyes and mouth opened wide, his breathing deepened. "If we want this to be a book, I must know the details," he insisted.

Brian hesitated, then raised his chin. "Let's just say it has to do with stolen furniture."

Carl's face relaxed. He frowned and shook his head. "That sure doesn't sound like book material to me. You must be working on something more important." Carl pressed against Brian's left arm, stopping him from mouthing the last of his hot dog. "Maybe you got a desperate plea over the phone?"

"No, but we just solved a mystery involving Indian bones and the Lancaster Convention Center." Brian smiled. "Now that was one for the books, if you know what I mean."

Persistence was one of Carl Rutter's traits. That's why he came to recover and destroy possible evidence described on the phone by John Mason. Carl studied "Sammy's" face as he said, "Didn't someone phone you yesterday and leave a message describing a crime?"

Brian shook his head. "Sammy didn't say—" Brian hesitated and started again. "I, Sammy, didn't receive a message on my phone." Brian looked up and to his right. "No, I don't recall any message on my phone."

Carl tried again. "Where is your cell phone? I don't see it on you."

Brian didn't have a phone of his own. He hesitated as he tried to adjust to the fact that he was pretending to be Sammy who did have a cell phone. He finally heard himself say, "I left it at home. I didn't want it to get wet in the rain."

They glanced at each other suspiciously.

A realization passed over Carl's hardened expression. *What a ploy!* he thought. *This guy is trying to secure an advantage over me. Brilliant! This kid is playing me like a puppet on a string. No way could this famous teenage amateur detective be this dumb. He saw right through my plan of pretending to be a writer. Well, Mr. Smarty Pants, I'll show you some strings that I can pull.*

Carl pushed aside his half-eaten hamburger and picked up the check. He smiled and motioned for Brenda. "Here, this is to pay for our food." He slid the check and the money toward the blond. Playing out his role as a writer, he said, "Brenda, I just decided Sammy Wilson here and his friend will be in my next book. I'm calling it *A Bird in Their Hands.*"

Brian said, "A better title would be *Brian Helm and Sammy Wilson, Super Crime-Fighters.* And I'm on the cover, wearing a flowing cape."

When Carl didn't reply, Brenda grinned

and winked at Brian. "Next your crime fighting adventures will be in the movies."

Brian beamed. He always fancied himself an actor. "Right. First a book, then Hollywood. They probably will want me to play myself." When Brian leaned back to promote his self-importance, his stool tilted backward. In desperation, he grabbed for the counter and missed, sending one flailing arm through the sleeve of the airborne jacket. He landed on the floor, entangled in the nylon. He scrambled to his knees and maneuvered his free arm through the remaining jacket sleeve. "Okay, I'm ready to go," he said, uprighting the stool and pretending the preceding action was planned. He stood up and staggered toward the door.

Brenda shouted after Brian, "I see your curls. They're real cute."

The baseball cap lay askew on his head. The teen quickly repositioned it to recapture and flatten any exposed curls.

"You have some tricky moves there, Sammy," Carl said grinning, thinking it was all an act. "Get in the car. I'll take you home. I'm going to my office to check out newspaper articles describing your past exploits."

Carl followed the teen to the car. The sky was a gray slate but free of rain. Carl shrugged off any doubts he had about his mission. Soon the amateur detective would be dangling by his strings and would give up the message. Carl marveled at the phony act the famous Sammy Wilson was putting on for his benefit. *He's playing the part of an idiot perfectly,* he thought. *It's too bad that it will all be for nothing.*

After Brenda watched the two leave, the phone rang. It was Mrs. Wilson.

"Hi, Brenda. I'm trying to track down Brian. Is he there by any chance?"

"He just left. He was with a man who's going to write a book about the boys. I heard him say he was going to take Brian home."

"Okay, great. Thank you, Brenda," Mrs. Wilson said, feeling much relieved.

CHAPTER FOUR

Sammy Wilson and his father opened their umbrellas to dry by the side door before they entered the house. Mrs. Wilson never allowed wet umbrellas in the house. That was another rule that father and son had to observe to eliminate any later discussion about moldy umbrellas.

"I'm hungry. How about you?" Mr. Wilson said as he opened the refrigerator. "I'm going for ham and cheese. Want some?"

Sammy plopped down on a kitchen chair and reached for the bread. "Sounds good. Don't forget the butter and mustard."

As the two settled down to eat, Mr. Wilson said, "I don't understand why Detective Phillips wanted you and Brian involved in this case. This is the third time household furniture has been stolen while the Amish are at church. Why don't the police just stake out some Amish farms the next Sunday there is a church service?"

"The police have done that," Sammy said.

"Hundreds of Amish farmhouses are left vacant every other Sunday, while they attend church in their district. The police don't have the workforce to cover every farm in Lancaster County."

Sammy's father smiled. "So Detective Phillips wants you and Brian to watch all the other farms?"

Sammy sneered. "Yeah, right. Look, so far, three farms have been broken into on three different Sundays. Detective Phillips thinks there may be a further pattern to their operation. He hasn't found any, but he hopes that Brian and I can discover a behavioral pattern, if one exists."

Mr. Wilson went to the sink, poured two glasses of water, and placed one in front of Sammy. "The police must have collected some evidence," he said with concern.

"Clues are hard to come by," Sammy said. "Thieves wore gloves to eliminate fingerprints. The evidence, so far, is mostly truck tire prints and shoe prints." Sammy used a finger to wipe a glob of mustard from his lips, returning it to his half-eaten sandwich. "It's impossible to match the tire and shoe prints to burglars who might live in Maryland, New Jersey, or some place else in Pennsylvania."

The kitchen door opened, and Sammy's mother rushed in. "How can you men sit here eating when Brian's gone?"

Sammy saw the concern on his mother's face. "What do you mean he's gone?"

Mrs. Wilson's arms flailed about. "He's gone, missing, maybe kidnapped."

"Hey, relax," Mr. Wilson said, twisting around to face his wife. "When you called me on my cell phone at the farm, you said Brian got into someone's car. Even if you didn't know the man, maybe Brian did. Maybe it was a relative."

With urgency in her voice, Mrs. Wilson said, "After I talked to you, I called Brenda at the snack counter. She told me Brian was there with a writer. When they left, she heard the man say he was taking Brian home and then doing some research. I called Mrs. Helm, and Brian wasn't home. She assumed he was here with Sammy."

"Your mystery man is a writer?" Sammy said.

"That's what Brenda said. He was going to write a book about you boys. Do you know of such a person, Sammy?"

Sammy shook his head and grinned. "No, but Brian is probably somewhere talking the man's ear off."

"I'm still worried," Mrs. Wilson said.

"Mom, so far, there isn't anything to suggest that Brian is in any danger."

Sensing that Sammy and her husband might be right about Brian, Mrs. Wilson took a deep breath and shrugged. "Maybe," she conceded.

Mr. Wilson stood, grabbed his empty plate, and went to the sink. "Sit and eat something. I'll watch the store."

"It's okay," Mrs. Wilson said. "Martha's there. She's working part-time today."

Sammy disappeared into the living room. Moments later he yelled, "Hey, Mom, where's my rain jacket?"

Mrs. Wilson was at the table assembling a sandwich. "I gave it to Brian to wear this morning when it was raining. Why? Do you need it?"

"No, but I think I left my cell phone in the inside pocket yesterday."

CHAPTER FIVE

B rian's sense of smell adapted to the aroma of straw and manure. But being tied to a wooden post in a barn was belittling to the young boy's pride. The cotton clothesline that held his upper body firmly to the post afforded little movement. A separate rope bound his hands together at the wrists.

The farm, like many others that Brian had visited, was a dairy farm. The flooring was wood with bales of straw stacked nearby, waiting to be used as bedding for the cow pens. Cows had to be milked twice a day, but Brian saw no cows on the farm.

An eerie feeling added to Brian's confinement. The barn was quiet, too quiet.

The teen's body jerked as the cooing of a roosting pigeon emphasized the silence. *Where were the farmer and his helpers? Where were the cows?* Brian wondered as he covered his eyes to make it all go away.

"Cut the act, Sammy. Take your hands away

from your face. I know you're not as stupid as you pretend," Carl said, leaning over Brian, who was bound to a heavy support post. "I have two men waiting for my phone call. What I tell them depends on you. If you tell me what John Mason said on the phone, I'll tell them to take no action. If you don't tell me about the message, they will enter your parents' store, rough up whoever is there, and tear the place apart. So it's up to you. What do I tell them to do?"

Brian's knees quivered. *What would Sammy do in this situation?* Brian wondered. He thought of past cases that had succeeded because of Sammy's clever intervention. He had to think. After all, he was pretending to be Sammy.

Carl grabbed the lad's shoulder and squeezed. "Come on. What will it be? Do you want your parents harmed or not?"

Brian squirmed, trying to loosen Carl's grip on his body. He twisted and strained against his bonds, hoping to escape. This wasn't supposed to happen. After all, he was Double-Oh-Seven-and-a-Half. He would not give in to this monster. He glanced up at the sunglasses bearing down on him. Inspiration spread through his body as only Brian could experience inspiration. If only Sammy could see him now! He was about to use his new psychological method to disarm the bad guy. A method he created on the spot.

"Say something," Carl said and squeezed harder.

"Do you know what your trouble is?" Brian

said, willing to go full speed ahead, win or lose. "You need to relax and examine your problem. Your body is racked with tensions built up over the years. You need insight into your childhood." Brian had heard Sammy use that line. "Your parents abused you as a child. You were bullied at school. Kids made fun of you because you were different. Your parents kept you locked up in a dark room. Your meanness and deceit is the result of years and years of imprisonment. You tied me up, acting out the torture you went through as a battered child." Brian nodded and smiled. "I just told you this, now you understand your problem, and your behavior will change. You can relax now and set me free." Brian smiled and extended his bound hands.

Carl stepped back, away from the teen. "Are you nuts?" he said. "My parents loved me. I did as I pleased. I was the bully at school, and I'm a bully now. Do you know why?" Carl said, moving his face within inches of Brian's nose. "Do you really know why?"

Brian closed his eyes and tilted his head to his right. "No, why?" he said, shaking, his voice strained.

"I'm a bully because I can be a bully, you little twerp, and because I want to be a bully. Now, what did John Mason say to you in the phone message?"

The bowl of soup that Mrs. Wilson had mentioned earlier visualized in front of Brian. Boy, did he want to be home eating that soup. "Okay," he said, "I'll tell you the truth. I'm not Sammy Wilson. I'm Brian Helm. I wasn't with Sammy the last couple of days, so you'll have to ask him about the phone call from your Mr. Mason."

Carl pointed to the rain jacket and baseball cap on the barn floor near Brian. "Ha, nice try, but I saw your name on your coat."

"That jacket isn't mine. Sammy's mother didn't want me to get wet, so she let me use Sammy's jacket and cap because it was raining."

Carl ran his tongue over his teeth as he considered the possible truth in the boy's statement. "Your wallet, let me see it."

"I don't have a wallet," Brian said. "Call my mother. She'll tell you who I am." Brian told the man the number to call.

Carl used his cell phone and dialed. "Hello. Who is this?" he said when a woman answered.

Voice: "Sarah Helm."

Carl: "And you have a son named Brian?"

Sarah Helm: "Are you the man who took Brian in his car?"

Carl: "I might be. Who told you about that?"

Sarah Helm: "Mrs. Wilson called, wanting to know if my son was home. She told me about you. She said you are a writer."

Carl: "Yes, I'm writing a book about Brian and Sammy. I'm going to bring your son right home. We just went for a bite to eat. So relax and describe your son to me. I need it for the book."

Sarah Helm: "Brian's a good Christian boy.

He can be impatient at times. He's always tinkering with things. He—"

Carl gritted his teeth. "No, no, Mrs. Helm. I want you to describe his appearance."

Sarah Helm: "He's a clean boy. He keeps his hair cut. He has soft teeth but he brushes them every night and day. He wears—"

Carl tried to restrain himself by biting his lower lip. "What color is Brian's hair?"

Sarah Helm: "Isn't he there with you? Take a look at him for gracious sake."

Carl: "I didn't want to tell you this, Mrs. Helm, but I'm color blind."

Sarah Helm: "Oh, you poor thing. Why, brown. My boy has brown hair. It's wavy. When it gets wet—"

Carl plodded on. "What color are his eyes?"

Sarah Helm: "Hazel. Some people say brown, but I say hazel."

Carl: "Does he have a small mole on the left side of his nose?"

Sarah Helm: "Oh, yes, it's a beauty mark, you know."

"Your boy will be home soon," Carl said, confused, but satisfied with her answers. He flipped the phone closed and returned it to his pocket.

Brian grimaced and strained against the rope. "I told you I'm Brian. Didn't I?" the teen said. "Now untie me and take me home before you get into serious trouble. My father's a lawyer, you know."

"Okay, so you're Brian, which explains your

strange behavior. You're staying right here until I get what I want. When Sammy knows I have you, he will give up the recorded message and forget about what it says."

Brian shook his head and kicked a leg up high. "Oh, no, he won't. He'll come here and have you arrested."

"How can he do that? He doesn't know where you are, and I'm not going to tell him. Are you? You don't even know where you are." Carl laughed and hurried to the barn door. "I'm going out and look around to make sure we're still alone." He checked his watch. "It's almost three. I'll be back soon and don't expect help. This place is closed down for months until the will is settled. No one lives here. The nearest farm is way down the road. Yelling won't help you. There are no cows grazing outside, and only corn is growing in the fields. But cheer up. You have hay bales and mice to keep you company."

CHAPTER SIX

The idea hit them all at the same time, but Sammy spoke first. "If Brian is wearing my jacket, and my phone is in the pocket, that solves our problem, Mom. We'll call my cell number, and then we'll know where Brian is."

"Yes, yes," Mrs. Wilson said and reached her hand over to the phone on the kitchen wall. She searched for Sammy's number, written on a list posted nearby, and dialed.

Sammy moved closer to the phone, repeating his number to make sure his mother had dialed it correctly.

Mrs. Wilson nodded. She twisted strands of hair around her finger. Her plastic-rimmed glasses slipped a notch down her nose. "It's ringing," she said. "It's ringing."

Their faces were blank with anticipation.

She slumped, fearing the worst, and said, "No one is answering."

The suspense continued as Mrs. Wilson dialed again.

CHAPTER SEVEN

Brian was alone in the barn, and still tied to the wooden post. He heard a small plane flying overhead. Pigeons fluttered about on the wooden ledge above. Luckily, the pigeons weren't directly above him. The partly opened barn door allowed the newly arrived sun to streak across the floorboards and over Sammy's cap and jacket.

Brian had smiled earlier as he was being tied with the rope. He knew a secret that every amateur detective had in their escape kit. If you expanded your muscles while being tied, the rope became loose later when you relaxed your muscles.

Brian had stood tall, flexed his muscles, and inhaled deeply to expand his chest as the rope was tightened around him and the post. Later, Brian discovered that with his muscles relaxed and lungs collapsed, the rope was no looser. He frowned at the thought, then wondered if weightlifting might help him in the future.

Now, alone in the barn, he wiggled and

stretched, trying to free his body. After much effort, his hands still remained tied in front of him and his upper body tied to the post.

Then he heard it.

Ringing bells.

Coming from the wooden floor. Coming from Sammy's jacket.

What is this about? Brian wondered. *Why is the jacket ringing?* Then Brian recognized the sound. He had heard it before: his partner's cell phone. *Did Sammy leave his phone in the jacket?* Brian couldn't recall any additional weight when he wore the jacket. *How much did a rain jacket weigh? How much did a cell phone weigh? Not much.* Brian shivered as another thought swept over him. *Had Sammy listened to the mysterious recorded message on the phone? Maybe the message was recorded overnight while the jacket hung lifeless in the dark closet.*

Brian heard the sound of shoes crunching on the gravel some distance from the barn. Was it Carl coming back, or was it someone else? A glimmer of hope sparkled in his eyes. Maybe Sammy had come to rescue him.

The ringing started again.

Oh, no! Please don't start ringing again, he thought to himself. *I don't want Carl to get his hands on the phone.* Restrained by the rope, Brian could do nothing to relieve his curiosity concerning the new, never-ending ringing. He had to reach the phone. He had to let someone know where he was before Carl entered the barn.

He lifted one leg in the air, but that got him no closer to the jacket. Even if he had something that could reach the jacket, his hands were tied together.

The ringing stopped.

Brian froze, but his eyes roamed continuously from the jacket to the barn door.

Waiting.

Carl entered the barn and gazed at Brian. He panned the barn as though looking for someone else. "I heard a ringing in here. What was it?" Still glancing around, he walked toward Brian.

"That was me," Brian said.

Carl put both hands on his hips. "You were ringing?"

"Well, no, I was . . . whistling," Brian said and tried to imitate the sound by whistling notes similar to the ringing phone.

"I don't recognize the tune," Carl said sarcastically. In a childish voice, he added, "Ah, I bet you were whistling for your dog, Lassie, to go and fetch Sammy."

"I'm nervous. I whistle when I'm nervous. I can't help it."

"Well, I'm nervous, too," Carl said. "I didn't intend to hold you in this barn, but you gave me no choice. If you hadn't misled me into thinking you were Sammy Wilson, we wouldn't be here. I'd be talking to Sammy. He'd explain the message he received from John Mason, and it would all be over."

"What is so important about the message? Did you commit a crime, and this Mason guy is snitching on you?" Brian said.

Carl's eyes opened wide. "Dumb kids like you think you know it all." Carl flipped his hands aside. "It's nothing," he said. "Just something that happened years ago."

"How can it be nothing when you have me tied up in a barn over some dumb recorded message by a dumb person on a dumb phone?"

Carl raised his voice. "It's only dumb to kids who are dumb . . . and stupid."

Brian nodded. "I may be dumb, but I know your name and what you look like."

The man waved his hands in the air. "Hey, dumb kid, my name is not Carl Rutter, and I'm not a writer." He aimed his index finger at his own face. "Can you really describe me? Are you going to say, 'He was of medium height, medium weight, wearing a droopy hat, dark sunglasses, and a fake mustache?' The police will love that."

Brian glanced hard at the hair beneath the man's nose. "The mustache looks real. So it's really a fake?" he said.

Without answering, the man shook his head, picked up a glass jar, and walked away from Brian.

The young detective tried again to squeeze free of the ropes, but it wasn't to be.

"Ah, here it is," the man said, stooping over a faucet on top of a three-foot pipe sticking up from the floor. Water gushed out and into the jar. Some water splashed onto the wooden floor and ran down between the cracks.

The floorboards reminded Brian of a case they had solved: *Secret Under the Floorboard.* "Hey, I know a young Amish boy who hid books under a loose board in the barn. If books were hidden there now, they would be soaking wet."

"Carl" stooped and peered down through the cracks. "Just dirt and stones down there. What did you expect, hidden treasure?" He stood up and rinsed the jar again before filling it and offering it to Brian. "Here, drink . . . and don't expect food. The water should hold you until I get back."

Brian's hands were still tied at the wrists, but he was able to pivot his fingers enough to hold the jar of water.

As the man walked away, he taunted Brian with, "I don't know about you, but I'm hungry. I'll call Sammy after I eat a steak sandwich at the Bird-in-Hand Family Restaurant. If your friend gives me what I want, I'll be back soon. If not . . ." He shrugged. "Who knows when?"

"Sammy won't tell you anything, you big thug," Brian said.

"He will if he wants you back," the man yelled over his shoulder as he strolled out the barn door and closed it.

The banging door rattled the pigeons, causing them to flap about. When they finally settled down, the stillness and the quiet returned, reminding Brian how isolated he was. He didn't feel like a superhero at the moment. He raised his head, tipped the jar to his lips, and took a drink. The teenager shivered as he saw specks floating about in the water. The water, dirt and all, still gave him encouragement.

The jacket and cell phone were still on the floor several feet away. If only he could reach the jacket and drag it toward him. *There has to be a way,* Brian thought. *If Sammy were here, he would know how. He would . . . What would he do?*

Brian was ready for another swallow of water. He looked at the jar, and then down at the rope that held him to the wooden post. He could drop and break the jar on the floor and use the broken glass to cut the rope, but he couldn't bend to reach it. He glanced closely at the clothesline rope. He visualized his wet undershirts. *Most cotton cloth expanded when it was wet,* he thought. *Would clothesline made of woven cotton strands do the same?* He remembered how his mother's clothesline drooped when soaked after a rainfall.

Brian spilled the water over the many strands of rope that bound his chest to the post. He did it slowly to allow the water to soak in.

Then he waited.

After several minutes, he inhaled and pulled himself away from the post. He strained forward like a team of mules pulling a plow. He repeated the exercise two more times, then he stopped and relaxed.

It worked! The wet rope had stretched!

The question was, had the cotton rope given way enough for him to squirm down and out from under it? Holding his bound hands high above him, he shimmied down through the stretched rope.

It was enough!

He was free, except for his hands, but that didn't matter. He picked up the jacket and spread it out gently on the floor. He patted it until he felt the small phone in the inside pocket. That was his lifeline to freedom. He handled the phone carefully. A broken one would not help him. He flipped it opened and dialed Sammy's home phone number.

He got a busy signal.

He waited and dialed again. "Come on. Come on," he said out loud.

The encouragement didn't help. The busy signal was heard again.

CHAPTER EIGHT

Sammy's parents went back to managing their store business, leaving him at the kitchen table. Surely the phone would ring soon, letting them know that Brian was okay. The super sleuth couldn't bring himself to believe his friend was in any real danger. However, the potential was there. According to Brenda, Brian was with a writer, Carl somebody, who said he was taking Brian home, but didn't. Now what? Sammy sat at the table and played with the saltshaker. *Who would want to kidnap a fifteen-year-old teenager, and why?* he wondered.

The phone rang.

The aspiring detective took a deep breath, pushed his chair back, stood, and grabbed the phone on the wall. He heard the voice before he had a chance to speak.

Voice: "Hello, Sammy Wilson?"

Sammy squinted as he tried to recognize the voice, and then said, "Yes."

Voice: "Last night, did you receive a message on your cell phone from John Mason?"

Now Sammy was confused. He had expected to hear something concerning Brian. "Who is this?" he said.

Voice: "I'm a friend of John's. He died last night in the hospital. He died after a long illness. He was mentally unstable. He imagined strange things. I was with John when he died. He was delusional. I'm afraid he was acting out a fantasy in the phone message he sent you. I just wanted to warn you not to rely on anything John Mason said in his message. Do you know the message I'm talking about?"

The teen listened intently, but didn't hear anything pertaining to Brian. The name John Mason did sound familiar though. "No, I don't know about any message, but I haven't checked my phone for messages today." Sammy wondered if the message had anything to do with Brian. "By the way, are you the man Brian Helm was with this morning at the farmer's market?"

Voice: "Ah, no. I don't know a Brian Helm. I'm Doctor Eshelman. John Mason had been under my care for the past two years. I study terminally ill patients concerning their illusions, fantasies, hallucinations, and such. I'd be willing to pay you three hundred dollars for your phone containing the message. It would really aid my research."

The offer of money caused Sammy to pause. Why would a doctor who's doing research not ask for a copy of the message? Why ask for the entire cell phone? Most research is financed by grants, making money scarce. No, there was something wrong here. Sammy eased back into the chair and leaned his elbows on the table. "Well, right now, I'm more interested in locating a friend of mine, Brian Helm. After I find him, I'll be glad to talk to you about John Mason and your research program."

Voice: "I'm afraid that won't do. I want the information now."

That did it for Sammy. He had nothing to lose. "Then let's get right to it. You tell me about Brian, and I'll give you the message."

The voice took on an animated tone. "So you know what the message says?"

Sammy was playing this by ear. He had left his phone in his jacket overnight and had no chance to examine it. He played along and said, "Yes, I listened to it."

Voice: "And?"

"And what?" Sammy said.

Voice: "What do you intend to do about it?"

Sammy wanted more information. "I'm not sure yet. What do you think I should do about it?"

Voice: "Nothing, absolutely nothing. Above all, don't tell anyone where she is. She doesn't want to go back."

"Okay, then if what you say is true, you bring Brian back, and I'll give you the phone with the message for *five* hundred dollars." Sammy wanted to give the impression that he was more interested in money than pursuing what John Mason had to say in the message.

Voice: "And you'll disregard the message and take no action."

"If what you say is true, it's garbage anyway. So why should I waste my time on a dead-end case?"

Voice: "Well, then, we have a deal." The voice became calm and reassuring. "I'll give you Brian and five hundred dollars, and you'll give me the phone containing the message."

"Where will we make the exchange?" Sammy said.

Voice: "I'll drive by your house in one hour. You give me the phone, and I'll give you the money and tell you where Brian is. Don't think about calling the police, or I'll have my men show up sometime and tear apart your parents' store. They won't care who they hurt in the process. Do you get the message?"

"If you don't release Brian," Sammy said, "I'll call the FBI, inform the local police, and post John Mason's voice confession on the Internet. Do you get my message?"

CHAPTER NINE

The phone was still busy. Brian had to get out of the barn fast. He wasn't sure when "Carl" would return. He clamped the baseball cap over his hair, grabbed the jacket, and ran to the door, which opened with a simple push. He blinked. The sun was bright. It felt strange trying to juggle the items with his hands still tied together.

He squinted and scanned the area. He saw fields of corn. A vine-covered old propane tank sat next to the farmhouse. He could get lost in the corn. The tank was closer and would make a good enough cover in case "Carl" returned. Brian ran and ran, holding the jacket and phone clamped between his hands. He skidded on his back to a stop among some vines behind the propane tank. He sat up, shook off some dirt, and hurriedly redialed his friend. This time Sammy answered.

"Hey, Sammy, it's me," said Brian, the words pouring from his mouth. "A man took me to this barn. He tied me up. He wanted to know about a message left on your phone. I didn't know your phone was in your jacket pocket. I have the phone. I'm calling you on it now. The message must be important. Do you know John Mason? That's who put the message on your phone. What should—"

"Brian, slow down," Sammy said, interrupting his friend. "I already know about my phone and the message. I just talked to the man who took you. Where are you?"

"He had me tied up in a barn, but ropes can't hold me. I used my—"

Sammy rolled his eyes. "Brian. Tell me where you are."

"I escaped from the barn. I'm hiding behind a big propane tank near the farmhouse."

Sammy pounded on the table with his hand. "Brian, where is the farm?"

Brian rose up on his knees and glanced around. "I don't know where I am," he said.

"Why don't you know where you are?" Sammy said.

Brian hesitated. "After we left Brenda's Snack Counter, the man told me to get into the back seat of his car. He said that I should lie down and close my eyes."

"So, just like that, you did what he said?"

"Well, yeah."

"Did he have a gun?"

"No."

"Then why did you do it? Why didn't you run away?"

"He said I should close my eyes because he had something special for me. Then he drove around the back roads until we came to this farm."

Sammy squirmed in the chair. "Okay, we have to find out where you are. Take a look around you. What do you see?"

"It's a farm," Brian said. "Nobody lives here now. No cows. Nothing except corn growing in the fields."

"Okay, so it's a vacant farm," Sammy said. "Is it an Amish or an English farm? Do you see any electric wires coming into the farm?"

"Yeah, I do now, and I remember wiring and lightbulbs in the barn."

"So it's an English farm. How long were you riding in the car?"

"Not long. Maybe five minutes."

"You're still within the Bird-in-Hand area," Sammy said. "Think, Brian, did the man say anything that might be a clue?"

"Oh, I got it. I got it," Brian said, greatly excited. "Before he left the barn one time, he said it was almost three o'clock."

"And?"

"After that, I heard a small engined plane pass over the barn. All you have to do is check with the Smoketown Airport. Find out who was flying a plane in the Bird-in-Hand area and where they were around three o'clock."

"Brian, you're a genius . . . occasionally,"

Sammy said, "but closing your eyes in a stranger's car, waiting for a surprise, is stretching it."

"Hey, you know how I like surprises," Brian said.

Sammy quickly shifted back to business. "I'm also going to check around to see what farms are vacant and maybe up for sale."

"Uh, oh, here comes the black car up the lane."

"Stay where you are," Sammy said. "Don't move. We're on the way. Don't lose the phone!"

"Make it fast," Brian pleaded. "Goodbye."

Brian nudged the phone shut with his chin, hugged the ground, and slithered under the metal tank. Normally, Brian would have enjoyed playing hide-and-seek, but now fear ruined the moment.

*****

Seeing the barn door wide open, "Carl" ran from the car and into the building. Seconds later, he exited the barn, looked around, and shouted, "I'll find you, Brian! I'll find you!" He turned in a circle, then he stopped and listened. Hearing no sounds from his freed hostage, he drove off in his car. He spent the next half-hour scouring the backcountry roads, searching for the teenage boy who was his ticket to the recorded message. The next question was, what would he do if he didn't have Brian to exchange for the message?

CHAPTER TEN

"Oh, Brian, you're back!" Mrs. Wilson shouted as she rushed from the back room of the Bird-in-Hand Country Store. With the help of real estate listings and the Smoketown Airport, Sammy and his father narrowed the search down to the Johnson farm. They found Brian cowering behind the propane tank, just as they had imagined.

"I'm trained to get out of situations like that. Right, Sammy?" Brian said.

"I think you just proved it," Sammy said, feeling relieved that his friend returned safely.

A relaxed Brian, in a joyful mood, stood tall and tugged his thumbs behind his belt. "Yeah, I used the old water-on-the-rope trick."

"I use that all the time," Mr. Wilson said, winking at Sammy.

"You do?" Brian said.

"Sure, when my wife has me 'fit to be tied,' I throw water on her."

Sammy laughed, while his mother stuck out her tongue and made a face at her husband. Brian, still shaky from his experience, produced a mechanical smile.

Sammy noticed his baseball cap on Brian. "You can wear my cap until your hair is dry," he said, and threw his rain jacket at Brian. "Come on, we have a lot to do." He held his cell phone up in the air. "You hang up the jacket while I get the phone ready up in the bedroom. I'm eager to hear what a dying man has to say."

CHAPTER ELEVEN

S ammy's second-floor bedroom window overlooked Main Street, otherwise known as Rt. 340 and the Old Philadelphia Pike. Right now, the super sleuth was not interested in watching the tourists, the Amish, or vehicles merging in the street below. He was hungry, but dinner could wait. The cell phone was open, recharged, and ready to reveal its mysterious message.

The bedroom was small with a wall-to-wall bookshelf. A bed was against the opposite wall which displayed problem-solving, award-winning certificates and a *Baltimore Orioles* baseball pennant. Many news articles announcing Sammy and Brian's crime-fighting adventures were tacked to the bulletin board on the end wall. An old oak desk sat in front of the bookshelves, facing the bed. It supported a computer, a printer, and the cell phone. It also supported Brian as well. His right foot touched the floor, keeping his body perched on the corner of the desk. Sammy, sitting behind the desk, activated the cell phone speaker.

"Sammy Wilson . . . this is . . . John Mason . . . No time left . . . I kidnapped . . . a girl . . . June 14, 1995, . . . but not . . . what you think . . . investigate . . . to understand . . . I gave her to . . . Henry Hershey and . . . wife . . . blue dog . . . ahhhhhh."

Brian sat mystified, listening as John Mason's last breath left his body. Sammy was trying to relate this message to what "Carl Rutter" had said to him earlier over the phone: "She doesn't want to go back."

Sammy reclined with his hands clasped behind his head. "Wow, he didn't say much, but what he did say was explosive."

Brian stood, faced Sammy, and folded his arms across his chest. "John Mason kidnapped a girl back in 1995."

Sammy sprang forward in his chair and raised a finger. "Yeah, but he said that it's not what we think."

"How can he kidnap someone and it not be a kidnapping?" Brian said, backing up to the bed.

Sammy stretched and brushed his straight dark hair back away from his blue eyes. "That's what we have to figure out, Brian."

Brian flopped back across the end of the bed, his feet dangling down toward the floor. "Did I hear him say he gave the girl to someone named Hershey and a blue dog? Do dogs come in blue?"

"Let's listen to it again."

"Sammy Wilson . . . this is . . . John Mason . . . No time left . . . I kidnapped . . . a girl . . . June 14, 1995, . . . but not . . . what you think . . . investigate . . . to understand . . . I gave her to . . . Henry Hershey and . . . wife . . . blue dog . . . ahhhhhh."

The ceiling above Brian represented a place of obtainable answers, but at the moment, the ceiling was out of order. He was on his own. "I don't see what's to investigate," Brian said. "The problem is simple. Mr. Mason kidnapped a little girl and gave her to Henry Hershey and his wife. We go to the Hersheys and take the girl back home."

"That happened 15 years ago. We do need to investigate," Sammy said, "to find out the name of the girl and where her family lives. We need to know when and why Mr. Mason gave the child to the Hersheys. Also, somewhere among the transaction is a blue dog.

Brian said, "I never saw a blue dog. This is going to be one of those cases where the more we investigate, the more we need to investigate. Dead ends will be all over the place. We'll be interviewing people forever, and what will we have in the end? A blue dog and a kidnapped girl to take back home."

Sammy ignored his buddy and lined up his chair with the computer monitor. He went online and typed into the search engine: kidnapped June 14, 1995. A list appeared, but only one item was of interest to Sammy. He clicked on it and read the information to Brian.

Rose Marie Maxwell

Eight-year-old Rose Marie Maxwell was taken from her home on the 600 block of Broad Leaf Drive, Harrisburg, PA. She was last seen playing in the side yard of her house at 2:30 p.m. June 14, 1995. She was 4 feet high and weighed 70 lbs. When last seen, she was wearing a white T-shirt and shorts with a floral pattern. She has blond hair and blue eyes.

No evidence relating to Rose Marie's disappearance was ever found. A non-family member may have abducted her. None of the neighbors noticed anything unusual in the area at the time she vanished.

After 15 years, Rose Marie Maxwell's disappearance still remains unsolved. Her family still lives in the house where she lived in 1995.

Sammy studied the six photos that accompanied the article. According to the captions, they showed Rose Marie from two to eight years old. Two pictures were taken in her bedroom, two in other rooms of the house, and two outdoors.

The super sleuth clicked the print button

and made three copies. He put one print into his desk drawer. He folded the second copy into a paper airplane and sailed it over to Brian on the bed. "Here, Brian, catch."

Brian glanced up and grabbed at it, plunging the airplane into a wrinkled nosedive. "Ah," he said, "airmail. When you care enough to send the very best."

"Study that information and the pictures, Brian. Anything could be a clue," Sammy said. He kept the third copy for himself.

After looking over his crinkled copy, Brian said, "They have no idea who took her, but we know. Right, Sammy?"

"It would seem so," Sammy said. He read over the printout again. When he was finished, he said, "Okay, John Mason took the girl and then gave her to Henry Hershey and his wife. That raises some questions. Why did Mason take the girl? No ransom was asked for, so he didn't do it for money. Later, he gave the girl to the Hersheys. Why would he do that?"

Brian answered, "Maybe he stole the girl for the Hersheys. They couldn't have children. So Mason sold them one. Maybe he *did* kidnap her for money."

"Good thinking, Brian," Sammy said, trying to enhance his friend's self-esteem.

Brian smiled and said, "Could be that Mason needed money. He took the girl and sold her to Hershey."

Sammy shook his head. "That doesn't sound right. If Mason needed money, then why not demand ransom? That brings up another question: Was Rose Marie's family rich? We have research to do and questions to ask. That's why Mason wanted us to investigate his recorded confession."

Brian's neck muscles ached. He relaxed his head back onto the bed and looked at the ceiling for comfort. "Are we going to tell Detective Phillips about this?" he said.

Both the boys and Detective Ben Phillips of the local police department relied on each other to help solve cases. Many times the boys solved small cases before they became big headaches for the police department. Detective Phillips, in turn, provided the law enforcement and physical backup when needed by the boys.

Sammy thought deeply, then he said, "No, we won't tell Detective Phillips until we do some investigation. However, I am going to ask him to do a criminal background check on John Mason and Henry Hershey. We'll see what happens after that."

Brian's eyes followed a crack in the ceiling until it reached the bookshelves. One book caught his eye, *The Confessions of the Guilty*. Brian grimaced, picturing John Mason dying, and said, "If John Mason wanted to clear his conscience before he died, why didn't he confess to the police or a priest? Why give us his confession?"

Sammy frowned and shrugged. "Maybe he knew the police didn't have the work force or the time to give this case the attention that it needed. The law tends to see things in black and white. Either it's right or it's wrong. We, on the other hand, apply our hearts and emotions to add color to that black and white picture. Maybe that's what John Mason wants us to see, a complete picture in full color."

Brian sprang up from the bed and went to the window. He peered down at the activity below. He was looking for a black car with a driver wearing a drooping hat. "What about 'Carl,' our mystery man? He said he had two men who will attack your parents and wreck the shop."

"I doubt he will," Sammy said. "He's trying to create fear by using threats. We won't fall for it, but we do need to keep our eyes open just in case."

Brian turned from the window. "He was willing to kidnap me to get to your phone and the message."

"He had an agenda," Sammy said. "He didn't want us to hear John Mason's confession. By now, he knows that we have listened to it. He had a reason why he didn't want the message heard. Something in that message is harmful to him. We need to know what it is."

Brian went back to staking out the people below. Suddenly, he hesitated, smiled, and said, "I know. 'Carl' was a partner in the kidnapping. That's it. He and John Mason were in it together."

Sammy stood and, with head down, started a trip around his desk. "It's possible, and it's a reasonable assumption," he said. "Our mystery man expected John Mason to name him in his confession. He was going to be exposed as a kidnapper, so he had to do something. That something was to stop us from acting on the confession."

"So, right now, he's a loose cannon," Brian said, returning his attention to the street below.

Sammy stopped and rested his hand on the back of his chair. "We must identify this man soon."

"Can I eat first? My stomach is growling at me," Brian said.

Sammy checked his watch. "Yeah, go home. Be back here at 9:00 tomorrow morning."

"How do we start to find this man?" Brian said.

"We start with a list of everyone who was in the hospital room when John Mason made the phone call."

Brian stood at the door and said, "How do we get the names?"

Sammy sat at his desk, opened a drawer, and reached for the phonebook. "We talk to the one person who would have been there."

CHAPTER TWELVE

Mrs. Emma Mason lived on Mt. Sidney Road, right off the Old Philadelphia Pike. After one and a half days of rain, the boys felt liberated to be riding their bikes along the sun-covered rolling hills of Bird-in-Hand. Brian's hair had dried into "manly waves" instead of "girlie curly." Sammy's cell phone was back safe in his pocket. The day was starting out on a bright note. Nothing could dim their enthusiasm . . . except the black car that trailed one block behind them.

Mrs. Mason, wearing a light blue sweatsuit, opened the door and ushered the boys into her living room. The room was disheveled, with newspapers and magazines lying about. Dust had gathered on the end tables and the television set. A large framed photograph of her and her husband lay face up on the sofa. The glass was stained with fingerprints and dried tears.

Strain and months of worry etched extra years into her forty-five-year-old face. She was still an attractive woman with brown hair, dark eyes, and a fit body that any physical trainer would applaud.

"The house is a mess. Sorry, but my husband—"

Sammy interrupted by raising his hand and saying, "Hey, it's no problem, Mrs. Mason. We understand, and we're sorry about the loss of your husband."

Mrs. Mason gathered up newspapers. "It was a blessing he died. He suffered so, but, you know, with God's grace, you survive what life gives you. I have friends coming soon to be with me." Mrs. Mason offered a sheet of paper to Sammy. "Here are the names you wanted. When you called last night, I wondered if you were the Sammy Wilson my husband had last talked to. He died, you know, right after he phoned you."

"Yes, I know," Sammy said. "Thank you for the list."

Emma Mason touched Sammy's arm. "I'm curious. What did my husband say to you?"

Sammy could hardly reveal that her husband was a kidnapper. Unless she already knew? Being unsure, he answered, "He said he was dying and wanted Brian and me to keep investigating the bad guys."

She frowned. "John's dying, and with his last breath, he tells you to keep after the bad guys?"

Sammy looked at the paper in his hand. He couldn't tell her the truth. A white lie would have to do. "Well, there is more to it. He wanted us to get the names of people who were present when he died."

"Why?"

Sammy hated to continue the lie, but he wanted to establish how much Mrs. Mason knew about the kidnapping. He studied the woman carefully as he said, "It does sound odd, but your husband wanted us to send the list of names to *Rose Marie*."

The woman didn't flinch or openly react to the name. She innocently said, "Who is Rose Marie?"

Brian jumped in. "Maybe Rose Marie is a lawyer, and your husband wanted to reward everyone who was by his side when he died. Right, Sammy?"

Mrs. Mason shook her head. "We have no money. After the hospital bills are paid, we will be in debt."

"To tell you the truth, Mrs. Mason, I'm not sure why your husband called me. However, Brian and I will do our best to investigate and find out about this 'Rose Marie.'" Sammy felt less guilty after making that statement.

Mrs. Mason picked up the framed photograph from the sofa and said, "This is all too much for me." She collapsed on the sofa and let out a deep sigh. She waved at the love seat covered with a blanket. "Sit down, boys. Do you want something to drink?"

Sammy shook his head. "No, we're okay. We won't stay." He waited and then said, "Did you and your husband always live here in Lancaster County?"

"I did, but John didn't," Emma said. "He lived in Harrisburg."

"Oh, really," Sammy said, glancing at Brian. "I have an aunt living there. What street did he live on?"

"I don't remember. Something like Oak Tree or Maple Leaf Drive. We went back to visit once, several years ago."

"It wasn't Broad Leaf Drive, was it?"

"Yes, I believe it was."

"When did he move to Lancaster?"

She looked up and to her right. "1994. He was a school teacher. Did you know that? That's how we met. I taught at the same school." She gazed at the photograph and tears rolled down her cheeks. "We were married two years later, in 1996," she said, hugging the frame.

Sammy glanced at the names on the paper. "Do you know Henry Hershey and his wife?"

"Why, yes, we're good friends. We played cards . . ." Sadness crept into her voice. "We played cards with them up to the time John's cancer got out of control."

"Do they have any children?" Sammy said, then he held his breath.

"They have a daughter. Why do you ask?"

"I might know her. What's her name?"

"She got married a couple years ago. Her married name is Mary Tilson."

Sammy saw the light at the end of the tunnel. "Is she about twenty-three years old and lives in New Holland?"

Mrs Mason scratched her forehead. "The age is about right, but she lives in Manheim."

"Do you know her street address?" Sammy said, pressing his luck.

"No, I don't. My, you ask many questions for such a young boy."

"We're amateur detectives, kind of like cadets. We ask questions when we investigate. That's what your husband wanted." Sammy glanced down at the paper she had given him. "I see you didn't include the Hersheys on your list of names."

Mrs. Mason sat up straight. "They were there with John earlier that day, but not when he died. Do you think John would have wanted them included on the list?"

Sammy slipped a pen from his pocket. "I'm going to add their names. Do you know their address?"

"Charlotte Street in Millersville. I don't know the number."

Sammy stood and back-stepped to the door. Brian followed. "We'll go now. Thank you for the information you gave us," Sammy said. "I'm sure Mr. Mason would be pleased. Oh, before we go, what do you know about the blue dog?"

Mrs. Mason shook her head. "I only saw a blue dog once, and that was in a cartoon on television."

"Okay, thanks again," Sammy said.

Mrs. Mason stood by the door and waved as the boys mounted their bikes and rode away. As an afterthought, Mrs. Mason yelled, "When you find out, tell me about Rose Marie!"

CHAPTER THIRTEEN

Because the boys were fifteen, too young to drive a car, they had to rely on their parents for distant trips. Otherwise, they rode their bikes. After the boys got back home, they enlisted the help of Sammy's father to drive them to Charlotte Street in Millersville.

Millersville was a college town outside of Lancaster City. Charlotte Street was a long, curved, pleasant street sporting middle-class family homes. The Hersheys lived in a brick rancher with a plain lawn in front and a parking area around back.

A black car was parked in the driveway.

The teens left Mr. Wilson in the car and approached the house.

Brian couldn't believe it and pointed, "That's the car. It's the same one 'Carl' drove."

"Are you sure it's the same one?" Sammy said.

"Yeah, see the Penn State sticker on the

side window," Brian said, slipping around behind Sammy. "I remember that. It's the same car."

Sammy headed up the narrow concrete walk and said, "Let's find out who 'Carl' really is. Are you ready to walk into the lion's den?"

Brian was reluctant to follow. "'Carl' is Henry Hershey. That's who he is."

"He has a motive," Sammy said, stepping up to the front door. Before he rang the bell, voices were heard from inside the house.

Voice #1: "You're going to prison. Do you want that? Look, they can't do anything."

Voice #2: "Somebody will find out. It's out in the open now."

Voice #1: "If they find out, they find out, but don't help them. Just keep quiet."

Voice #2: "If only John didn't . . ."

Voice #1: "Keep your trap shut, and it will work."

Since Brian and he were out in the open, Sammy hated to wait any longer. He pushed the small, round, white button. "Well, now, let's see who opens the door," he said to Brian, several feet behind him. "If you think he's 'Carl,' cough, and then I'll know."

Brian looked back to check if Mr. Wilson was watching from the car. He was. Brian swallowed hard and waited for the door to open.

It opened slowly. A medium-size man appeared. He had a head of springy light-brown hair that made his head look top heavy. In Brian's eyes, his round, wire-rimmed glasses, small gray eyes, and thin nose created the image of a mad scientist.

Sammy didn't hear a cough from Brian, so he concluded the man was not "Carl," the mystery man. "Are you Henry Hershey?" he said.

"Yes, yes. What do you want?"

Sammy tried to see into the house past Mr. Hershey. He was eager to identify the second voice they had heard, but he saw no one. "I'm Sammy Wilson, and behind me is Brian Helm. We received a message from John Mason before he died. He told us about you." Sammy studied the man for a reaction. He wasn't disappointed.

Henry Hershey opened the door wider and stepped outside. He glanced up and down the street, then he focused on Mr. Wilson in the car.

"He's my father," Sammy said. "He's waiting for us."

"Come inside, quickly," the man said. He followed them in and closed the door. "I'll be right back." He went into the next room and probably elsewhere to confer with the other person in the house. When he returned, he said, "I'm alone. My wife is at work. I work at night."

I bet you do, Brian thought as he looked around for the cellar door. He imagined the "Mad Doctor" bending over steaming test tubes, gloating as he wrings his hands and hears shrieks through the night. *Ah,* Brian thought, *he created the world's first blue dog.*

Henry brought Brian out of his daydream when he added, "I'm night auditor for the Marriott Hotel in Lancaster."

Sammy was hoping to get Mr. Hershey to open up and tell the story of the kidnapping. He wanted to give the impression that he and Brian already knew the details, so he said, "John Mason confessed to the kidnapping of Rose Marie and your part in it. Now, I'd like to hear your side of the story."

"John did what?"

"Just before he died, he confessed to kidnapping a girl and said you were involved."

"That's crazy. Who heard this confession?"

"Brian and I did."

Henry frowned, his eyes squinting at the teenagers. "Do the police know about this confession?"

Sammy raised his shoulders. "Not yet."

"Why did he tell you two kids? You're teenagers, right? John must have lost his mind before he died."

"Are you saying that you don't know anything about the kidnapping of Rose Marie Maxwell?"

Henry nodded and said, "Right. I hate to say this, but John was out of his mind to say what he did. He was sick, really sick, when he died. My wife and I were there to visit him. He was talking crazy stuff."

It was time to raise the bar. "Then who is Mary Tilson?" Sammy said, trying to catch Henry Hershey off guard.

Henry drew back, his faced drained white. He hesitated before he spoke. "She's my daughter. Why?"

A car's motor started outside. The boys glanced at each other, glanced at Henry, and then hurried to the window. By that time, the black car was headed up the street. In seconds, it was gone.

So was "Carl."

Sammy turned back to the man, who was wiping his brow with his sleeve. "Who was that?" Sammy said. "Who owns the black car that was parked in your driveway?"

Mr. Hershey shrugged and said nothing.

"You know who it was. We heard you two talking in here before we rang the doorbell."

"Oh, that was a carpenter who is going to bid on remodeling our kitchen. He left by the back door." Henry stomped to the door and opened it. "If you want to ask any more questions, see my lawyer." He pointed his hand outside. "Now, why don't you boys go out and play ball or something and leave false confessions to the psychiatrists?"

Sammy took another stab at the confession. "Before he died, John Mason mentioned the blue dog."

"Yeah, the one you keep in your cellar," Brian added.

"I have no blue dog, or dogs of any color," he replied and waved the teens out the door. He watched Sammy and Brian heading for the car.

The blue dog, he thought. *I wonder where it is?*

CHAPTER FOURTEEN

Mrs. Mason thought that Mary Tilson, the Hersheys' daughter, lived in Manheim. She was right. The telephone book listed a Michael Tilson living on Doe Run Road. Sammy and Brian were confident that Henry Hershey would warn his daughter about the two teenagers. If that were true, she would be prepared for them on their arrival at the appointed time.

Later that afternoon, Sammy's mother provided the transportation to Manheim. She remained in the car and watched as the boys were abruptly allowed into the two-story brick house on Doe Run Road.

The woman before them was tall, had a round face, and was thirty pounds overweight. Her body projected contempt. She was hardly the shy eight-year-old shown in the pictures. A lot can happen in 15 years to change a person. She could be Rose Marie. The first tip-off was the blond hair and blue eyes. The second was her admitting to be the

Hersheys' daughter. The third, she appeared to be about twenty-three years old.

As the boys sat on the sofa, Brian knew their mission was ending. Sammy knew it was only beginning.

To reject the boys would only prolong their intrusion into her private life. Mary Tilson seemed ready to face their accusations. She adjusted her position in the chair as she fiddled with her uniform to avoid wrinkles. "I'll be going to work soon," she snapped. "This will have to be quick." She, indeed, was prepared for their visit. Her strategy was to keep the visit short and be ready for a quick exit.

Sammy didn't waste time. "As I said earlier, we're amateur detectives and are trying to locate Rose Marie Maxwell. She was kidnapped 15 years ago. We believe you are that person." Boom, bang, there it was, sweet and simple. Sammy waited for a reaction.

"What kind of detectives are you?" she said. "Do I look like I'm being held captive? No. Am I ready to dash out the door and head back into the arms of my 'real' mommy and daddy? No."

That was the question that had haunted Sammy after talking to Mrs. Mason. If Rose Marie now was a married adult, living unshackled, why didn't she run back to her real parents?

"You're right, Mrs. Tilson. We made a big mistake," Sammy said, wanting to appear he believed her. "That's an interesting uniform. What work do you and your husband do?"

The woman glanced at her watch and stood. "I'm a nurse, and my husband sells houses. I'm sorry, but I'm not the person you are looking for." She stood and nodded toward the door. "Now that's it. I must get ready for work. Goodbye."

"Did you know John Mason, who died recently?" Sammy said.

"I believe he was a friend of my parents."

"And the blue dog?"

Mary paused and glanced at the stairs leading to the second floor. Her eyes returned to Sammy as she said, "If John Mason had a blue dog, I never saw it. That's it. Goodbye."

Sammy saw the recognition on Mary's face at the mention of the blue dog. He cringed as he stood. "Could I use your restroom before we go?"

"Oh, if you must, but make it quick." She pointed. "It's up the stairs to the left."

Sammy hurried up the steps, entered the bathroom, and closed the door. He waited 5 seconds and looked back out and down the stairway. Brian had gone into action downstairs. He diverted Mary's attention to photographs displayed on the wall, while Sammy quickly scouted out some rooms upstairs. He hated to invade other people's property, but he could see no other way to bring justice to the case.

The guest room looked undisturbed. The bed was attractively adorned with an Amish quilt. Blue curtains at the windows complimented the blue of the quilt.

Sammy listened. Brian was still babbling away downstairs.

He dashed into the master bedroom. The bed was covered with a simple spread. The same blue-colored curtains were at the windows. One end table had a lamp, a phone, and a pair of reading glasses. The other table had a lamp, a paperback novel, and pills.

Outside the master bedroom, in the hall, were three opened cardboard storage boxes. They were stacked like bureau drawers and appeared to be waiting to be delivered to Goodwill. Upon inspection, Sammy discovered they contained folded bath towels—new bath towels.

A strip of paper protruding from a towel caught Sammy's eye. When he lifted a layer of the towel, he saw it was a hundred-dollar bill. He lifted the cloth higher. More bills were lined side by side. He quietly shifted the boxes to check the other towels. All were layered with new hundred-dollar bills. No way were these boxes going to Goodwill.

The bottom box contained something extra. Pushed to one side was something rolled up in a hand towel. As Sammy touched the towel, a piece of paper fell away. A line of numbers was written on it, ending with a separate four-digit number. Before he could unravel the hand towel, he heard Brian's voice. It came as a warning.

"Hurry up, Sammy!"

Sammy heard someone starting up the steps. He quickly re-stacked the boxes and rushed into the bathroom. He flushed the toilet, ran the spigot water, and headed for the stairs. He met Mary coming up.

Mary Tilson took a deep breath and herded the teens out the door.

When the boys were on the sidewalk, Sammy stopped and told Brian about seeing the money in the boxes containing towels. "Each towel had, I figured, ninety-six bills between the folds. Four bath towels per box equals thirty-eight thousand dollars, times three boxes equals over one hundred thousand dollars."

"Wow, that's not bad for a cloth bank," Brian said.

"What if she had more towels in the linen closet?" Sammy said. "She could be hoarding over a quarter million dollars."

"Ah, ha," Brian said. "Maybe she won the money on a racehorse named Blue Dog."

"Either that or she had the winning numbers in the lottery," Sammy said. "I saw a series of numbers written on paper in with the money."

"Hey, that's why she doesn't want to return to her real parents," Brian said.

Sammy shrugged and gave Brian a quizzical look.

"It's simple," Brian said. "Her parents told her never to gamble."

CHAPTER FIFTEEN

At 7:00 that evening, the boys were back in Sammy's room. Brian claimed his territory by lying across the bottom half of the bed and was skimming the article on Rose Marie's disappearance. He was preparing to brainstorm with Sammy.

Sammy was behind his desk, using the computer, listing what he knew about the case.

```
            JOHN MASON'S CONFESSION
     IF TRUE
John Mason kidnapped Rose Marie Maxwell.
John gave or sold girl to the Hersheys.
The Hersheys raised a girl named Mary Hershey.
Mary Hershey married and now named Mary Tilson.
Her description and age matches Rose Marie.

     IF FALSE
John Mason lied because of sickness. All was a
fantasy, including blue dog.
```

Inferences: John Mason kidnapped the girl because he confessed to it; Henry Hershey's only child is Rose Marie Maxwell, because Mason said he gave the girl to Hershey; Hershey's married daughter, Mary Tilson, is Rose Marie Maxwell, because she has blond hair and blue eyes and is about twenty-three years old. "Carl" and the blue dog is anybody's guess.

Which raises the questions: Why doesn't Rose Marie return to her real parents? How long has she had the money, and where did it come from?

Sammy pushed his chair back away from the desk and took a deep breath. He rubbed his fingers on his forehead and said to himself more than to Brian, "Where do we go from here?"

Brian, talking to the ceiling, said, "We tell Detective Phillips. He'll know what to do."

"Not yet," Sammy said. "We have to continue our investigation for Mr. Mason's sake."

Brian raised his head to look at Sammy. "What else is there to investigate?"

Sammy waved a hand in the air. "Did you forget about 'Carl,' the man who kidnapped you? He wanted the recorded message to disappear. He had a reason for his actions." Sammy reached into his pocket for the names Mrs. Mason had given him that morning. "'Carl' has to be a man who was in the hospital room when John Mason died. How else would he know about the message?"

"Is the name Carl Rutter there on the paper?" Brian said.

Sammy checked again. "No, there are only two men's names. Thomas Mason, John's brother, and Earl Landis, a friend, it says here. The other names are women, none of which I would consider suspects. I'll get the men's addresses. We can visit them and check out their physical appearance and see which one has a black car."

"With Penn State on the window," Brian added.

"Brian, we also need to find out why Rose Marie hasn't returned to her original parents."

Brian sprang up on the bed and said, "Oh, oh, I know. Remember several years ago, another kidnapped girl was found walking with her kidnapper on the street? She didn't try to escape either. It was something about her bonding with her kidnapper."

"Yes, that's right," Sammy said. "It could be true in this case, I suppose. Rose Marie was 8 years old. At that age, children are trying to develop their own identity. Her younger years were taken from her. The Hersheys held her and over time showed her love and kindness. She identified with the Hersheys and adopted their way of life and remained loyal to them."

"Couldn't she still want to visit her real parents to at least let them know she was okay?" Brian said.

"Maybe not, because the real parents would

press charges against the kidnappers. She, by now, is so bonded to her new parents that she wouldn't want them to go to jail."

"That makes sense," Brian said, collapsing back on the bed and returning his attention to the ceiling.

Sammy noted the main points he made on the computer and said, "We need to interview the Maxwells. We could use more clues."

Brian visualized Rt. 283 on the ceiling. "They live in Harrisburg, an hour's drive from here," he said.

"I'll check with Mom and Dad. One of them will take us. Can you be here at 10:00 in the morning?"

Brian nodded. "I'll be here."

"Good," Sammy said, "I'm curious to see the parents who Rose Marie is willing to ignore."

CHAPTER SIXTEEN

The next morning, Sammy sat on the low wall that separated the store's parking spaces from his house. Cars filled the small parking area in front of the store. The sun was splitting its seams, causing the "quilt of the day" to be absent from the store's window. Faded quilts didn't sell well.

A red car pulled in back of a car already parked in front of Sammy. *That's not right,* thought Sammy. *No double-parking.*

He hopped up off the wall as the car door opened. When the driver emerged, Sammy was face-to-face with Mary Tilson.

Her bulk was overwhelming as she grabbed Sammy's shoulders and shook him. "I want my money back," she yelled.

Sammy raised his arms and thrust them outwards, separating Mary's hands from his shoulders. "What money?" he said, still feeling the pinch from Mary's fingers.

"The money you took when you were in my house yesterday."

Sammy visualized the hundred-dollar bills tucked inside the towels. "I didn't take any money from you," he said.

Tourists and locals were starting to gather. Mr. Wilson emerged from the store. He very seldom interfered with his son's confrontations, unless his son's life was in danger. This time he stood by in case he was needed.

Mary Tilson continued, waving her finger. "You were the only person upstairs in my house yesterday. Unless I get the money back, I'm going to call the police. When they check for evidence, I wonder whose fingerprints they'll find all over my storage boxes?"

Since Sammy had not taken the money, he understood what was happening. She wanted to eliminate him as a problem by accusing him of robbery. He called her bluff. "Did you see any money in my hands when I came downstairs? I didn't steal your money, so here, use this." He extended his cell phone, knowing she couldn't afford to expose her hidden money to the Internal Revenue Service. "Go ahead. Call the police."

Mary Tilson glanced down, and then came up with a new angle. "You and Brian were the only people in my house yesterday. The bedroom window was open. You dropped the money out the window. Then you picked it up outside after you left the house."

"It won't work, Mrs. Tilson," Sammy said. "I'm sorry, but you'll have to go elsewhere to find your thief."

Mary noticed people staring. "It was you, all right. I'll be back." She got into her car, backed up, and sped away.

Mr. Wilson stepped forward. "Any problems?" he said as the red car vanished going west.

Sammy backed up and sat on the wall again. "There are problems, but I didn't make them mine. That was Mary Tilson, who we think is the real Rose Marie Maxwell. It's her parents we're going to see in Harrisburg." Sammy glanced to his right. "Brian should be here soon."

Sammy's father crossed his arms over his chest. "What do you hope to learn from the Maxwells?"

Sammy looked up at his father. "Why the Maxwells' daughter won't make contact with her real parents."

CHAPTER SEVENTEEN

The car made a sweep of Broad Leaf Drive. The suburb had a variety of house styles with prices ranging from two to five hundred thousand dollars. The address they looked for ended at the most expensive house on the block.

Mrs. Thelma Maxwell welcomed the boys into her home. Her thin figure and clothes reminded Sammy of a model. Her face wasn't as kind. The kidnapping aftermath left its mark, and reoccurring memories added more wrinkles. Underneath it all, Sammy saw a hardness.

Before entering the house, Sammy had expected sadness to coat its walls and tears to dampen its carpets. He was wrong. He saw no tears or sadness, only anger.

After hearing that the teenagers were Sammy and Brian, the famous amateur detectives from Lancaster County, Mrs. Maxwell agreed to answer all their questions. Evidently, the criminal cases solved by the boys did not miss the Harrisburg media. However, Mrs. Maxwell was not impressed enough or kind enough to offer the boys a drink or a seat.

The furnishings inside matched the wealthy image outside. Leather-covered furniture dominated the living room. An oriental carpet and a large, original abstract painting over the fireplace added class to the otherwise ordinary interior.

"Have the police or FBI turned up any clues as to where your daughter might be?" Sammy said.

"No, they are all incompetent," Mrs. Maxwell barked as though disciplining a child.

Because of Sammy's behavioral knowledge, her attitude did not surprise him. "If your daughter came back tomorrow, what would you do?"

She hesitated, then said, "My daughter is an adult now. We would treat her as a grownup."

How sad, Sammy thought. He visualized her shaking hands with her daughter as they were reunited.

Stretching across the picture window valance were many stuffed toy dogs. Even the bookshelves on either side of the window displayed the same.

The dogs fascinated Brian. "I see your dog collection is large. Is that in memory of your daughter?" he said.

Mrs. Maxwell smiled. "Oh, that's my collection. I always loved dogs. My daddy had two dogs when I was a child. I never had a dog of my own. A dog bit my husband when he was a boy. He won't allow a dog in the house. Except these." She swept her arm across the room. "My dogs are stuffed and don't bite."

Sammy saw the obvious answer to one of his puzzling questions. He said, "I bet Rose Marie had her own stuffed blue dog that she played with."

"No, no, that blue dog was mine. She took it," Mrs. Maxwell said with a touch of bitterness. She grabbed Sammy by the arm and said, "How did you know Rose had the blue dog?"

"It was just a guess. With so many stuffed dogs in the house, I figured she had one of her own."

"Why did you say it was blue?"

"Blue is my favorite color."

Mrs. Maxwell's voice softened. "Rose Marie loved that blue dog. She played with it and took it everywhere she went. So if you find Rose Marie, the dog will be nearby. As I said, it's mine." She motioned to an empty spot between two dogs up on the valance. "I'm saving its spot right there."

While Sammy had Mrs. Maxwell's attention, Brian took a dog from a shelf.

Sammy pointed out a black and white dog on the valance. Its glass eyes sparkled, and a shiny, pink tongue lay out of its open mouth. "That's a very unique dog," Sammy said. "Could I see it up close?"

"Oh, yes," Mrs. Maxwell said. She used a chair and white gloves to reach for the dog. She held the dog close for Sammy's inspection.

At the same time, Mrs. Maxwell saw Brian

returning a dog to the shelf. "Don't touch the dogs," she said sharply. "I don't like them touched. Oil from your hands can affect the synthetic hair. That's why I wear gloves when I handle them."

"Thank you, Mrs. Maxwell. It's a very unique dog," Sammy said, and then added, "Did you know a John Mason who died recently?"

"John Mason?" she repeated as she placed the dog back into its rightful position. She stepped down and sat on the chair while she stripped off the gloves. "I haven't heard that name for a while. He was a neighbor years ago, but he moved away."

"Before Mr. Mason died, he mentioned you and your husband," Sammy said.

"I must say, I didn't like him. He was nosey, always meddling into the affairs of others in the neighborhood."

"Is your husband at work?" Sammy said.

"My husband is upstairs sleeping. Sometimes he works at night."

"What kind of work is that?" Brian said.

"You may ask, but it's none of your business," came a voice booming from the elaborate curved stairway. "Why are you yelling when I'm trying to sleep? We've been through this before, Thelma. Haven't I said, 'No noise when I'm sleeping?' Now you bring boys in here. What's going on, Thelma? Tell me, Thelma, what's going on?"

Brian stepped back, ready to run to the door.

"I'm sorry, Leonard. This is Sammy and Brian

from Bird-in-Hand in Lancaster County. You know, the boy detectives from the police. They want to help find our daughter."

"Yeah, I know who they are," he barked, gripping the railing and slowly lowering himself to sit on a step. He slumped, placing his elbows back on the next step up. The fifty-year-old man's body was large and lacked exercise. He hacked a cigarette cough. The robe he wore fought to cover his rotund middle. The white vertical stripe of his undershirt announced the battle was lost.

The boys stared at the man, at his black curly hair turning gray at the temples, at his Roman nose and wide-set dark eyes. Brian thought the curls looked silly. Sammy thought that the Hersheys were a better choice of family for Rose Marie.

Leonard grasped the railing and, with some difficulty, pulled himself up. "Find my daughter and you'll suddenly become $10,000 richer," he announced with anger. He turned and struggled back up the stairs.

Sammy called after him, "If you want us to help you, Mr. Maxwell, we'll need to know what kind of work you do."

"Why?" he said with his back to them, still plodding up the last few steps.

Sammy answered, "Your boss or fellow workers might be involved in the kidnapping."

After Leonard reached the top step and disappeared around a corner, his voice bellowed, "There are no fellow workers. *I am the boss.*"

Thelma gathered the boys closer and whispered, "He's an importer. He buys things from China and Africa, places like that. He resells to customers around the country. Here. I'll show you." Thelma's tone was one of a spouse revealing secrets as revenge for her husband's cutting remarks.

Sammy and Brian followed Thelma to a building behind the house. It resembled a small warehouse. A transport truck was parked nearby. Inside, unopened boxes were stacked along a wall, and opened cartons were on long, wooden tables along the opposite wall. Miscellaneous merchandise was exposed for inspection.

A hefty, dark man, sitting at an old scarred desk, turned sideways and raised the largest hand Sammy and Brian had ever seen. His soft, gray eyes were almost swallowed up by his puffy face. "Whoa, that's far enough," he said, evidently not pleased to see uninvited guests.

"It's me, Butch," Mrs. Maxwell said. "Just wanted the boys to see the layout. They think there's still hope for finding Rose Marie."

"Give it up, Thelma," Butch said. "Rose Marie is gone. Get real and get the kids out of here. It's boss' orders." Then, standing, he physically shoved the trio out the door. "You want me to lose my job? Go on. Get out of here."

Brian glanced back at the carton boxes. He created images of illegal items that might be smuggled into the country. He made a mean face at Butch and then ran after Sammy.

Sammy shook off the rude handling and noticed, for the first time, a man sitting in the truck. His eyes were open but not active. With the commotion inside and out of the warehouse, Sammy thought the man should have reacted somehow by looking their way. The man never moved.

"Is the man in the truck okay?" Sammy said.

Butch laughed and laughed.

Thelma gave a short chuckle and said, "It's a dummy, a blown-up vinyl dummy wearing men's clothing."

Brian walked closer to the truck and looked in. The vinyl dummy was of a man with a 3-D ruddy face, having a projected nose and even ears. "Why is he in the truck?" Brian said.

"We got the idea from the cops," Butch said, sounding proud of the project. "It was in the news several years ago. The cops put a dummy police car near the highway. They dressed up a mannequin in a police outfit and placed him in the driver's seat. From a distance, the speeders thought they were being watched from a real patrol car. Boy, did they slow down."

"I remember reading that," Sammy said, and glanced again at the figure in the cab of the truck. "He looks real, but what's his purpose?"

Butch stared at Thelma.

She nodded and said, "It's okay. They know that Leonard's an importer. They were just talking to him inside. Go ahead, you can tell them."

"We have imports arriving on the west coast

and the east coast. The boss has an office here in Harrisburg and another office in San Francisco. We have customers all over the country. A driver leaves Harrisburg with merchandise for the office and customers out West. At the same time, another driver leaves San Francisco, carrying merchandise for our office and customers here in the East. The two truckers meet in Nebraska at a shopping mall and exchange trucks. Our driver takes the San Francisco truck back to Harrisburg. The truck from Harrisburg continues the trip to San Francisco driven by their driver."

"In other words," Sammy said, "you switch drivers in Nebraska, and each driver returns in a different truck containing different merchandise."

"You got that right," Butch said, "but that gave us problems. At first, some trucks were hijacked. Others were just driven away when the trucks were discovered parked at the shopping mall without a driver. You see, the two truckers didn't always arrive in the parking lot at the same time. There could be a difference of a whole day's wait by one of the drivers."

"I can understand that," Sammy said. "A truck might break down and make the driver late."

Butch smacked Sammy's back and said, "You got it, man. While the driver waits for the other truck to show up, he goes for a coffee break or eats or gets a room for the night. When he comes back, the truck is gone. Stolen. But, if a dummy is in the driver's seat, the truck is still there, safe, when the driver gets back. Also, the truck is less likely to be hijacked out on the road if the punks see what they think are two guys in the truck."

Sammy pointed to a man with thick black hair combed straight back, dark eyes, and a bushy mustache. He wore bib overalls and was kneeling in fresh dirt at a rose bush. "Is that man your truck driver?" Sammy said.

"Absolutely not. That's Garcia, the gardener," Thelma said. "He's reliable and friendly, but he's noisy," She waved at the gardener and yelled. "Garcia, get to work. You're paid by the hour."

Garcia, unfazed by her remarks, smiled and waved back.

"See what I mean by friendly?" Thelma said and added, "Okay, that's it. Back into the house. I wanted to give you an idea of the business. Though I don't understand how that will bring back my daughter."

Before Sammy entered the house, he glanced back at the gardener. A small camera protruded from his coverall bib. *Was the camera part of Garcia's gardening tools?* he wondered. *Pride of one's work could lead to photographs, and when attached to a résumé, might guarantee a job,* he thought. The reality of the situation led the super sleuth to believe that Garcia had taken photos of them for other reasons.

Back in the living room, Sammy said to Mrs. Maxwell, "I asked you about Mr. Mason, your previous neighbor, because he provided information about your daughter."

"What information? If Mr. Mason saw a girl with a blue dog, that's our daughter."

"He told us—" was all Brian could say before Sammy stopped him by saying, "We're in the process of investigating that. At the moment, we're not positive the information is accurate. We'll know later if it produces results. Brian and I wanted to meet you and your husband to compare present-day people to a fifteen–year–old mystery."

Thelma spread out her hands. "Well, here we are. You met us. Now go get our daughter back." She wore a sour expression as she led them to the door.

*****

It was Brian who surprised both Sammy and Mr. Wilson on the drive back to Bird-in-Hand. "Do you think that Mrs. Maxwell's stuffed dogs were all imported by her husband?" Brian said from the back seat.

Sammy twisted sideways in the front seat to see Brian. "Not all, but some. Why?"

"I was thinking that maybe there is more to the import business than stuffed toys. I bet he imports illegal stuff."

"He wouldn't be in business long if he did," Mr. Wilson said. "The government inspects imported goods and investigates people like Mr. Maxwell."

"They can't inspect everything," Brian said. "What if we analyzed the stuffing of one of the toy dogs?"

"How do we do that?" Sammy said.

Brian tilted his body and reached into his pants pocket. "I just happen to have . . ."

Sammy closed his eyes and shook his head. "Please don't tell me you took a dog."

"No, but my little fingernail fell through the stitching underneath the dog." Brian opened his hand to reveal threads of cloth-like material. "This stuff accidentally came out into the palm of my hand."

Sammy leaned over and put his nose into the material. "Smells like cotton or polyester to me."

Brian continued his theory. "Sometimes drugs are soaked into paper, cardboard, and cloth. When it dries the drugs are left in the material."

Mr. Wilson glanced up at his rearview mirror. "Do you think 'Mr. Importer' is into drugs?"

Sammy nodded. "Brian might have a point, Dad. We'll stop at the police station and have Detective Phillips examine the stuffing. Also, he was to check if John Mason and Henry Hershey had criminal records."

Sammy's father checked the rearview mirror again. "Any reason why a black car should be following us?" he said.

CHAPTER EIGHTEEN

The detective had kept the nineteen-year-old boy waiting alone in the interrogation room. When the detective did enter after thirty minutes, he carried a thick folder. The manila file looked impressive with its photos, charts, and written records sticking out.

The young man's eyes scrutinized the folder as it lay on the table before him. He shifted in his chair. The detective stayed standing, then taking his eyes from the folder, he launched into the interrogation of the suspect.

"Gregory, this folder has your name on it." Gregory saw that his name was, indeed, clipped to it.

"You have been sitting in this room for half an hour." Gregory agreed to that.

"You're wondering what information about you is in this file." Gregory was worried about what the police had uncovered about him.

With all two hundred twenty pounds and 6

feet 2 inches to back him up, the detective locked his dark, penetrating eyes on the teen. "You held the crying baby girl in your arms."

Gregory had held the baby, and it was a girl, and she was crying.

"Now tell me, did you shake the baby girl once or twice?"

"Only once. Honest, only once," Gregory said, pleading his case.

The detective nodded and said, "Thank you, Gregory." He produced a pad and pen. "Here, write down what happened and sign it. Someone will be here soon to take care of you." The formidable figure gathered the folder, walked out, and slipped into the next room.

"Well, did you recognize your method of interrogation?" Detective Ben Phillips asked the two boys in the room.

Sammy and Brian had been watching the proceedings from behind the two-way mirror. Several times they had used the same interrogation room to probe their own suspects under Detective Phillips' supervision.

Sammy spoke first. "You kept the suspect waiting alone for a time to build suspense. Then you arrived displaying a mock folder with his name attached. To his mind, the folder held the truth about him. You used the 'Yes Method,' where every statement you made was true. The suspect would have to answer yes to each statement. That set up a 'Yes' response. Then, you hit him with a double bind.

You gave him a choice between two alternatives: 'Did you shake the baby once or twice?' Either choice had him admitting he shook the baby. Of course, he selected the lesser of the two evils by saying he only shook the baby one time. That's all you needed: his confessing to shaking the baby."

Brian tilted his head toward the two-way mirror. "What's the story on him?" he said.

Detective Phillips gritted his teeth and said, "Gregory was babysitting. The parents came home and found their baby boy unresponsive. They rushed him to the hospital. The doctor reported to us that the baby had been shaken. The baby is okay now, but it looked bad for a while. Probably had a concussion. When Gregory was first questioned, he said he hadn't done anything to the baby. He said the baby hit his head on the crib. Well, you heard what he just admitted."

"Don't forget those piercing eyes of yours," Brian said. "They'll rip the truth from anyone."

Detective Ben Phillips' receding hairline and thin mustache followed his dark eyes as he leaned down toward Brian. "What crime did you commit today?" he said in a low baritone voice.

Sammy smiled and said, "Don't answer that, Brian. He'll put you away for ten years."

Even with the kidding, Brian felt guilty as he reached into his pocket and produced stuffing that he had extracted from the toy dog. "This is from inside a toy stuffed dog," Brian said. "The man imports stuff from Africa and China. I thought he might be importing drugs." Brian held out his hand. "Can you test this?"

Phillips bent over and smelled the material in Brian's hand. "I can't detect any drug smell, but let me have it tested."

Fifteen minutes later, Detective Paul Grossman stuck his head into Detective Phillips' office and said, "No trace of any drugs. Is that good or bad? Do I need to be aware of anything you boys are working on?"

Phillips glanced at the boys sitting on folding chairs in his cramped office. Sammy responded. "It's good, I suppose, but we're still investigating. We'll get back to you later."

Phillips raised his hand to Grossman. "Thanks for your report, Paul. I'll keep you informed if anything positive turns up soon."

In the 15 minutes they had waited for Grossman's test results, Detective Phillips stated that both John Mason and Henry Hershey had no previous convictions, no criminal records of any kind. This news deepened the mystery. Why would two decent citizens be involved in a kidnapping? Sammy and Brian had given Detective Phillips no details of their investigation other than that they were looking into a fifteen-year-old kidnapping case for a friend.

"What's the latest development in the Amish furniture theft case?" Sammy said.

"We traced the truck tire treads to a certain

Toyota truck model. We checked used furniture dealers in the area, but nothing has turned up."

Sammy said, "Here are my thoughts on it. What the three Amish farms have in common are their location near Rt. 30. The thieves are using the Rt. 30 bypass for a quick getaway. If you focus stakeouts on Sundays at farms along the bypass, you might get lucky."

"That's worth investigating. We'll give it a shot," Detective Phillips said. "Oh, and Sammy, when you're ready, will you fill me in on the details of your recent case?"

Sammy nodded. "You can count on it."

*****

Back in Sammy's bedroom, Brian bemoaned the fact that they had lost sight of the black car. It had faded away into the back traffic on Rt. 283. "'Carl' wants to keep us from finding out who he is," Brian said. "I'll say this, though, Leonard Maxwell is not our man, because 'Carl's' belly isn't that fat."

"Our mystery man has to be either Thomas Mason, the brother, or Earl Landis, a friend," Sammy said. "Both were there when John Mason died. I got their addresses last night. There might be an image of the men on the Internet."

In the search engine, Sammy typed *photo of Thomas Mason*. Several different men's photos appeared. Sammy clicked one at a time until a

Ronks Road address revealed their Thomas Mason, a restaurant owner.

Brian studied the face. He imagined it with a floppy hat, sunglasses, and a mustache. "I can't be sure, but I'd say no. That's not him."

"One more to go," Sammy said, clicking back to the search engine. This time he typed *photo of Earl Landis*. Again, photos of different men appeared, but the man who matched the address had a construction business and was not 'Carl.' He was an African American.

"Henry Hershey must know who owns the car. The car was parked in his driveway," Brian said. He squeezed his hands into fists. "That was our only lead. We should have gotten the license number before we went into his house."

"Yes, we should have, but we were too fast to assume that Mr. Hershey owned the car," Sammy said. "'Carl' must be the man who was in the house with Mr. Hershey. This third man must be involved in the kidnapping with John Mason and Henry Hershey. Who else would benefit from the kidnapping? John Mason maybe got money from the Hersheys. The Hersheys couldn't have a child of their own, so they paid Mr. Mason to get them one. Who else would have a reason to be involved?"

"Since Mr. Mason is dead, only Mr. Hershey knows, and he's not talking," Brian said, moving to the window.

The evening's fading light was throwing

its blanket over the little village of Bird-in-Hand, hinting that the lingering tourists should call it a day.

No black cars were in sight.

Brian moped to the bed and flopped back, causing the bed to squeak. After consulting the ceiling, he said, "Only one answer remains why Rose Marie won't contact her real parents. She's afraid they will report the Hersheys to the FBI. Maybe that's what John Mason wanted us to discover in our investigation."

Sammy sat in his chair, leaned back, and locked his fingers behind his head. "He already knew that when he was alive," he said. "No, Brian, something more was bothering him."

"It has to be the blue dog," Brian said, "or he wouldn't have mentioned it."

"I was just thinking, Brian. What if the blue dog wasn't a blue dog?"

"What do you mean?" Brian said too quickly. His face brightened. "Oh, you mean the 'Blue Dog' might be the name of a car or a football team."

Sammy added, "Or a restaurant or a racehorse, like you mentioned to explain the money Mary Tilson had."

Brian sat up and slid off the bed. He stood tall and, in his deepest voice, said, "Or a code word used by a secret agent to reach his operative in the field."

Sammy pointed to the bed. "Sit, Brian. 'Blue dog' could even be a computer password. We can go on and on. It's never-ending. We're right back where we started." Sammy glanced at his watch. "I suggest we adjourn until tomorrow."

Brian winced at the ceiling. "You're not giving up, are you?"

Sammy smiled and, in a rare humorous mood, said, "Brian, we never give up." Sammy stood and placed his hand over his heart. "Remember our motto: Never in the light of day or the dark of night, in the heat of the sun or the cold of winter, in the dryness of the desert or the wetness of a monsoon, in the—"

"Okay, okay, I get the idea," Brian said. "This case is getting to you. You're beginning to sound like me."

Sammy reclaimed his chair and breathed deeply. "I'm releasing some tension, that's all."

Brian stood and rubbed his hands together. "So what you're saying is, tomorrow we start a new day. Right, Sammy?"

"The people involved know we possess John Mason's recorded confession and that we have stirred the pot, so to speak. Now let's wait and see who make's the next move."

CHAPTER NINETEEN

"Carl" sat on a hay bale and counted the hundred-dollar bills. He created twelve ten-thousand-dollar bundles, which he neatly arranged in a tin box. One hundred twenty thousand dollars was stashed safely away. He smiled as he maneuvered the altered floorboard over the metal box and glanced up at the post that once held Brian Helm. "Well, Brian, thanks for the idea," 'Carl' said to himself and hammered the last nail into the flooring. "You escaped from me, you slippery bugger, but this money is going nowhere—until I get more, much more."

*****

At the same time, a man was allowed into the Wilson's house through the kitchen side door. He had shown a badge to Mr. Wilson. "Sammy, there's a man here to see you. He's from U.S. Customs. Should I send him up?"

"Yeah, send him up," said an unsure voice. Some scampering around was heard from the bedroom.

When the man walked into the room, Sammy and Brian were standing at attention. Their expressions changed from curiosity to surprise.

"At ease, men," the man said, smiling. He pulled out a leather wallet and flipped it open. "I'm Juan Garcia, U.S. Customs." He extended his hand. "Sammy Wilson and Brian Helm, I assume."

Sammy shook hands and said, "In this room, we try not to assume anything. We examine the facts."

"And rightly you should," said Garcia.

"I'm Brian," said Brian, shaking hands, wanting part of the action.

Sammy placed a hand on his chin and frowned. "Hmm, you look familiar, like the gardener for the Maxwells. So which is the real you, the gardener or a U.S. Customs agent?" Sammy said, knowing the answer.

"Ah, I wasn't sure you would recognize me," Garcia said.

"I'd know that mustache anywhere," Brian said and waved at the rocking chair. "Since you're a real customs inspector, you get to sit on the rocker throne."

"I know from digging into your backgrounds that you boys aren't always this fun-loving." He moved to the rocker and piled all the cushions onto the floor. He shrugged and said, "Now I don't know whether to sit on the floor or the rocking chair." He paused, then sat in the rocker. Switching to a serious face, he said, "What is your interest in Leonard Maxwell?"

"You took our picture, and you checked our backgrounds," Sammy said. "You know what we do, or you wouldn't be here, revealing your undercover work."

Garcia slid his hands along the rocking chair arms. "That's true. Now, are you saying that Leonard Maxwell is connected to your current case?"

"We are investigating the kidnapping of his daughter for a friend who died recently," Sammy said, and then turned the tables on the customs inspector. "What is your interest in Leonard Maxwell?"

"Let me start by saying 108 million maritime containers are used to import and export merchandise worldwide. They measure 8 feet by 8 ½ feet by 20-40 feet long. U.S. Customs inspects 10% of these."

"So custom inspectors only check one box out of ten," Brian said, wanting to show off his math skills.

"Right. We can't take the time to check more containers. If we did, the shipments would back up and create a mess."

"This is leading us to the importer, Leonard Maxwell," Sammy said.

"Correct. As I said, we can only inspect one carton out of ten. Somehow, some way, Maxwell is importing and distributing illegal products into this country."

"How do you know that?" Sammy asked.

"Because illegal drugs turn up in areas where his middlemen live."

"By 'middlemen' you mean the wholesalers who sell the merchandise to individual stores," Brian said.

Garcia nodded. "I know what you're thinking. Why don't we search his warehouse and trucks? Well, we do from time to time and find nothing illegal."

"You search his warehouse inside and out?"

"Yep. Same with the truck."

Sammy pictured the Maxwell warehouse he had seen. He pictured the large transport truck parked outside. He went through some scenarios, imagining how he would conceal contraband.

Brian recognized Sammy posture, the placid face, and motionless body. Sammy was in repose, free from mental stress, relaxed, searching for an answer to a problem. The twitching of Garcia's mustache caused Brian to raise a finger to his lips. Garcia nodded and returned the gesture, indicating his understanding to remain quiet while Sammy was thinking through the problem.

The sudden sparkle in Sammy's blue eyes signaled a conclusion. Sammy sat on the edge of his desk and faced Juan Garcia. "Did you ever examine the blown-up dummy in the truck?" he asked.

A shockwave went through Juan Garcia's

body. "Oh, gee," he said. Leaving the rocker in motion, he bolted for the door. "I'm out of here. Maxwell has a truck ready to leave at noon." As Juan ran down the steps, he shouted back, "Thanks, boys! I'll keep in touch."

Brian stood tall and saluted Sammy. "Chief, you did it again."

"Hey, not so fast. They might only find hot air in the dummy. Then who's going to look stupid?" Sammy said.

Brian waved a finger at Sammy. "You lied to Mr. Garcia. You told him we don't assume. Instead, we look at the facts."

"I didn't say that they would find anything in the dummy. I only asked if they had inspected it."

Brian snapped to attention again and saluted. "Sorry, I spoke without thinking, Chief. Of course, you are right again. Who am I to question your motives, to doubt your every word, not to follow you up the mountain of smartness, up the ladder to success, up the—"

Sammy rolled his eyes, passed Brian, and started down the stairs.

Brian quickly followed, saying, "Hey, you're going in the wrong direction. Up is the other way."

In the kitchen, Sammy said, "I'll see if Dad can drive us to Millersville this morning. Mr. Hershey said he worked at night as night auditor, which means he's home during the day."

Brian sat at the table and reached for the loaf

of bread. "We're going to make him confess. Right, Sammy?"

Sammy watched as Brian held a slice of bread on his flat palm. "What do you intend to do with that, keep staring at it?"

"There are all kinds of possibilities," Brian said. "I could put peanut butter on it if I had peanut butter."

After a quick search of the cupboards, Sammy found some.

Brian applied a generous amount of the peanut butter to the bread and stared at his creation.

"Now what?" Sammy said.

"This needs some jelly."

Sammy saw where this was going, so he smiled and pampered his hungry friend with a jar of grape jelly.

Brian spared no time in topping off the peanut butter with the jelly. He took a bite and frowned.

"Now what?" Sammy said.

"This would taste great with soup. Do you have chicken noodle?"

Sammy opened a can of soup, microwaved it in a bowl, and set the bowl and spoon before his friend. He put his face close to Brian and said sarcastically, "Now, do you mind if I sit and watch you eat?"

"Not yet," Brian said.

"Why not?"

"You haven't served my dessert yet," Brian replied.

"Brian, why do I put up with you?"

Brian grinned. "Because I'm likable, lovable, and I chew gum with my mouth closed."

Mr. Wilson came into the kitchen. "What was that all about with the U.S. Customs fellow? Something to do with Maxwell, I bet."

"They suspect he's importing and distributing illegal drugs," Sammy said.

"Can you and Brian help them?"

"I think we did," Sammy said. "I suggested they search the blown-up dummies they have in their trucks."

"Good call," Mr. Wilson said. "Where do you go from here?"

"To Millersville, if you're available and want to take us."

"Your mother and the part-time help are in the shop, so this is your lucky day."

"We want to talk to Mr. Hershey again. Now that we know more about his so-called daughter, I think another visit from us is in order. For instance, I wonder if he knows about all that money his daughter has hidden away?"

"That's the woman who came here and yelled at you for stealing her money?"

Sammy nodded and raised his eyebrows. "I must have left evidence up in her rooms that showed I had discovered her hidden money."

"She said her bedroom window was open," Brian said between bites. "That means someone climbed in and took the money."

"The window was closed when I was up there," Sammy said. "If it really was stolen, it happened after we left and Mary went to work. That means someone came through the window before she came home the next morning."

Brian pushed his soup bowl aside. "Her husband would have been there sometime after she left for her nigh shift. She said he sells houses."

"I wouldn't count on that," Sammy said. "Realtors work all kinds of hours. Ask our friend, Joyce Myers. Her father sells real estate."

Sammy's father reached into the refrigerator. "After I eat, we can go. I'm going to make myself some ham and eggs."

Brian glanced at Sammy, "Oh, I didn't know you had ham and eggs."

"Brian, don't even think about it," Sammy said.

CHAPTER TWENTY

His feathered brown hair and horror-picture image had not changed. For Brian, Henry Hershey was the evil scientist who created blue dogs in his laboratory. Sammy saw a different image. Henry Hershey, the hostile man that he was, had strong emotions. Fifteen years of guilt can create a protective behavior. The man had plenty to hide. Sammy saw Henry Hershey as ready to reveal all, if the super sleuth pushed the right buttons.

Sammy's job was to break through the hard shell and expose the sensitive and caring man who, years ago, just wanted to have a child of his own.

Again, the boys found Henry Hershey alone in his house, his wife at work. At first, Henry didn't want the boys in his house, until Sammy mentioned the money that his daughter had hoarded. Hershey then wanted to hear more. When Sammy described U.S. Customs' interest in Leonard Maxwell's import business, he softened. If Maxwell was tied up in his own legal battles, he might not be inclined to press charges against him.

"Mr. Hershey, we can prove that your daughter is Rose Marie, a girl kidnapped 15 years ago. We can do it with fingerprints and DNA. It's over, Mr. Hershey. If Rose Marie wants to go home, she no longer needs to fear retaliation from her real parents. They might be in jail soon."

"My wife and I will go to jail, too."

"It depends on your side of the story," Sammy said, "of your involvement in the kidnapping."

Henry paused as he held his hand to his mouth. "Before I tell you the truth, I need to know some things. Did John confess to the police?" He frowned, his eyes squinting at the teenager.

"No, he did not," Sammy said.

The frown continued.

Sammy pointed to a leather recliner. "Mr. Hershey, if you sit down, you can talk about it." This gave Henry the indirect suggestion that he would talk as a result of sitting in the recliner.

Reluctantly, Henry sat, but he did not recline.

Sammy started with, "First, who owns the black car? What's his name?"

"Now wait a minute," Henry said. "If you want to talk about the kidnapping and John, okay, but that's it. Anything else is off limits."

Sammy nodded and backed up onto a chair. Brian sat and balanced himself on a footstool.

"I want an answer," Henry said. "Why did

John Mason expose the kidnapping to you instead of the police?"

"Brian and I have the reputation for solving crimes in the Lancaster County area. We both are detectives-in-training, I guess you could say. John Mason heard about our work and how we operate. We try to be fair and understanding before we accuse anyone of a crime. Mr. Mason knew this. I believe that's why he wanted us to investigate and discover all the facts before the police got involved. Mr. Hershey, after fifteen years of holding it in, isn't it time for you to let it out?"

Henry leaned forward. "Okay, here it is. It wasn't a real kidnapping."

The statement shocked the boys.

The official police report and other newspaper accounts listed it as a kidnapping. Sammy was sure of that. "Why wasn't it a real kidnapping?" he said.

"Because it was more like a rescue," Henry said.

"A rescue?" Brian said, slipping off the footstool and landing on his side. He quickly remounted the wobbly footstool and said, "This is like riding a horse." Seeing Sammy and Mr. Hershey watching him, he added, "It's okay. I'm a fast learner."

Showing annoyance at the intrusion, Henry continued, "Look, when John lived in Harrisburg, his neighbors were the Maxwells, importers of who-knew-what. Many times John would see their little girl playing in the yard. The girl was Rose Marie.

According to John, she never smiled, was half starved, and was covered with bruises and cuts on her body. John told me that Mr. Maxwell had always wanted a boy. When they had a girl instead, he treated her badly. John called the authorities often, but nothing was ever done about the situation. Rose Marie was so afraid of her father that she would lie about how she got the bruises and cuts. She would say she fell down the cellar steps, that sort of thing. Later, Mary told us her father said he would kill her and her mother if she ever told the truth."

"Mary was the name you gave Rose Marie after the kidnapping," Sammy said.

"Yes, after the *rescue,*" Henry said, correcting Sammy.

Sammy shifted in the chair. "John moved from Harrisburg to Lancaster in 1994. Why did he wait a year before he went back to 'rescue' her?"

"John was a schoolteacher. He worked with children. He wasn't married then. John told me he couldn't get the suffering girl out of his mind. He had nightmares. In them, Rose Marie called out to him, asking for help. He knew my wife and I had wanted a child, but we could never have one. John had had enough. He made plans for the next summer. He went back to Harrisburg, saw the girl playing in the yard, and asked her if she wanted to get away from her abusive parents. She said she did and was anxious to leave."

"What about the blue dog?" Brian asked.

Henry looked up to his right. "John said she

ran back into the house to get it. It's been with her ever since."

Sammy continued. "Were you or anyone else connected to the actual kidnapping?"

"No, the rescue was John's idea. My wife and I were hesitant at first, when John suggested we take the girl. At the time, my wife and I were thinking about adopting a child. Then we saw Rose Marie, how she was hurting, starved for love, and grateful to anyone who showed her kindness. We took her as our own, knowing what the consequences would be. I still think we did the right thing."

Sammy frowned. "Rose Marie's parents might disagree with you."

Henry Hershey raised his eyebrows, smacked his lips together, and shrugged. "On the other hand, they might have been glad to be rid of her. They didn't report her missing for two days."

"Did Rose Marie give you and your wife any trouble growing up?" Sammy said.

Henry smiled. "The first three years were great. She appreciated everything we did for her. But she was a typical teenager. She put on extra weight, rebelled, and had her secrets. Peer pressure and all that. She was a private person. She graduated high school and went to nursing school. She married recently to Michael Tilson and is doing well."

"Which brings us to the money she has accumulated," Sammy said. "Any idea where it came from?"

"No, I'm as surprised as you are. We were

always able to provide for her. It's probably her husband's money."

"No, she told me it was her money," Sammy said. "Who paid for nursing school?"

Henry smiled. "She did. She worked and saved her money."

A familiar tingling sensation told Sammy that his subconscious was trying to get his attention. "Did she have her own bank account?"

"Yes, she did."

Sammy visualized the details banking entailed— checkbooks, deposits, withdrawals, ATM machines, and PIN numbers. "Brian, we're almost there," he said.

Henry shrugged. "I can't help you more." He trailed his finger along the arm of the recliner and looked up at Sammy. "What do you intend to do now that you've heard the complete story?"

"It's not complete until Rose Marie Maxwell tells her version of the story." Sammy sat back and closed his eyes, taking time to sort out information he had uncovered recently. It was an awkward pause. Finally, he stood, smiled at his conclusion, and raised his index finger. "When Brian and I get home, I'll call Mary and make an appointment to see her tomorrow. I think I'm on to something, but I'll wait to hear it from her."

"Do you know about the money?" Brian asked Sammy.

"Maybe, and I'm closing in on the black car," Sammy said, grinning.

Henry squinted at Sammy, but said nothing.

"I just have to check one thing," Sammy said.

"How do you know you have one thing to check?" Brian said.

Sammy's smile broadened. "Because one name was omitted from the list of those present when John Mason died."

CHAPTER TWENTY-ONE

Mary Tilson was visibly upset when she opened her door to the boys. "I know now that you didn't take the money," she said, stepping aside, allowing the door to open wider. "Look inside. What a mess. It was like this when I got home from work this morning."

Sammy and Brian carefully moved around items strewn on the floor. End table drawers were pulled out, their contents spilled on the sofa and the floor. This was more than vandalism. Somebody was searching for something of value.

"Every room in the house has been ravaged," Mary said, placing her hand on her forehead. "It's been searched, ransacked, and for what? My money was stolen days ago." She spread her hands in front of her. "And now this," she said.

"Was anything taken this time?" Brian said.

"Not that I noticed. My TV is still here. My jewelry is intact."

"They were searching for something," Sammy

said. "Perhaps they came back looking for more money."

"I have no more money. They took it all before."

A car horn sounded from the front of the house.

A man wearing a gray suit came running down the steps. "That's for me," he said as he kissed Mary and then acknowledged the boys. "You must be Sammy and Brian. I'm Michael Tilson, Mary's husband." His blue eyes and curly blond hair added to his good looks. "Sorry to be in a rush, but I'm late for work. Mary, I'll help you clean up when I come home after work. Goodbye."

The slammed door accented his whirlpool departure.

"He's like that all the time, aways in a hurry," Mary said. "He carpools with our neighbor."

"Does your neighbor sell houses, too?" Brian said.

Mary bent over and picked up a potted flower, trying to contain the soil within the broken planter. "No, he works at the bank," she said, placing the leaking pot on newspaper.

Brian checked the window. The car pulling away was blue, not black.

Sammy watched Mary carefully as he asked, "Henry Hershey told you, didn't he?"

"My father?"

"Maybe we should call him your foster father," Sammy said. "Yesterday, he told Brian and me the story behind the kidnapping, or the 'rescue' as he calls it."

Mary breathed deeply. "Yes, he told me that he told you. So now you know. Are you going to contact the authorities after you talk to me?"

"That depends on your answers to my questions," Sammy said. "Does your husband know about your history, that you were kidnapped?"

Mary nodded. "He knows. I told him after we were married."

"Now that you know Brian and I didn't take your money or make this mess, who would have a reason for doing it?"

She shrugged. "I don't know. I really don't."

"Somebody learned you had money," Sammy said. "Oh, before I forget, how much money was stolen?"

Mary hesitated, raising a hand to her throat. "Five thousand dollars," she said.

"Bong!" Sammy said unexpectedly and loudly. "That's not the true answer. It was more than $5,000. I told your foster father I would learn the balance of the true story from you. Will I?"

Mary trembled at the pressure being applied by the teenager. "How do you know it was more than $5,000?" she muttered.

Sammy couldn't confess his intrusion into her storage boxes, so he pointed to Brian. "My partner is a psychic. He knew that your answer was a lie. Three blinks with his right eye signals a yes. Three blinks with the left eye is a no."

Brian was taken aback by his sudden inclusion into the questioning. He quickly adjusted to the challenge. Most of his life was spent improvising—much to his embarrassment. He stood tall, mentally alert, developing the mystic character Sammy had made of him. He placed his fingertips on his forehead and wiggled his eyebrows.

Mary didn't know whether to laugh or be scared. "Nobody can know such things," she said. "It's baloney."

Sammy studied her for a moment. "Haven't you heard of psychics helping the police solve cases? The police don't think it's baloney. Let's try it again. How much money was stolen?"

"Ten thousand dollars," she said and glanced at Brian for a reaction.

Brian, knowing the real amount of money, blinked his left eye three times.

"Bong! Wrong answer," Sammy said. "Let's save some time here, Mary, or Rose Marie. Was the amount of money stolen more than $100,000?"

Mary again glanced at Brian, whose eyes were ready to render a verdict.

Unable to turn away from Brian, she said, "Yes, it was."

This time, Brian blinked his right eye three times.

"Ah, correct," Sammy said. "Let's continue. You kept calling it *your* money. Whose money was it, yours or your husband's?"

"Does it matter? The money was ours."

Shaking his head slightly, Sammy looked

at Brian. The teen picked up on the signal and blinked his left eye three times.

"All right, the money was mine," Mary answered, before Sammy made the annoying bong sound again.

"What was the source of all that money?"

Mary glanced from Brian to Sammy, then back to Brian.

"John Mason," she said.

Brian waited for a sign from Sammy, but none came. Sammy was deep in thought. Now that John Mason was dead, how could he prove that Mr. Mason had not given her the money?

Brian felt Mary's eyes continuing to test his revelations. He had to answer correctly or his psychic reputation would be weakened. So what else could he do? He blinked both eyes together three times.

"Ah," Sammy said, "both right and wrong." He scratched his head. "Now, what should I make of that?" he said.

"Make what you want, but it's true. John Mason gave me the money."

"Why? Why would Mr. Mason give you all that money?"

Before she could answer, the phone rang in the next room.

"I'll be right back," she said, kicking aside some items to make a path.

A group of plastic flowers landed on the steps leading upstairs. Several steps up, a hand towel lay partially opened, exposing a blue fuzzy stump.

Sammy pulled the towel away, sending its contents tumbling to the step below.

Brian and he gazed at each other.

The blue stump turned into the elusive blue dog—in mint condition.

Sammy switched his thinking to another important matter. "Brian, did you ever have a favorite toy when you were a kid?"

"Yeah, but it wasn't a toy dog. It was a dump truck. I'd fill it with stuff and push it all around the house."

"Ever play with it outside?"

Brian's smile widened as he used his hands to illustrate his words. "That was the best, using dirt. I'd scoop it in, push the truck a couple of feet, and dump it out. It made a big pile of dirt."

"Where is that truck now?" Sammy said.

"In a cardboard box somewhere, I guess. I don't think it works anymore. I know one wheel is missing." Brian looked suspiciously at his friend. "Why did you want to know?"

Mary's loud voice disturbed the moment. Evidently, the telephone conversation was not a happy one. The tone of Mary Tilson's voice suggested that her problems were not over. Whoever was on the phone was demanding something of her, which, if Sammy and Brian had heard her repeat it correctly, was the last of her money—$200,000.

Mary came back into the room crying.

"What's wrong, Mrs. Tilson?" Sammy said.

"It's terrible, terrible. My husband has been kidnapped," she said.

CHAPTER TWENTY-TWO

Sammy refused to believe it. The scenario was not as he had imagined. Ever since Brian and he had returned home, Sammy had to make adjustments to his earlier assessment. According to Mary, the caller demanded $200,000 for the return of her husband unharmed. She had one day to get the money. He would then contact her with further instructions.

On Sammy's insistence, Mary called her husband's place of business. They confirmed that he had not shown up for an open house appointment. They hadn't seen him all day. She called his cell phone, no answer. Next, she phoned her neighbor at the bank. He said he had dropped her husband off at the open house sign.

What worried Sammy was that Mary made no hesitation about getting the money. She had over $100,000 stolen from her and now $200,000 more was not going to be a problem. *What's going on here?* Sammy wondered.

Brian was rambling toward the ceiling. "Does she keep all that money in the house?" he said as Sammy snapped out of his daydream.

Sammy had his face buried in his arms, folded on the desk. "Maybe," he said, "or she withdraws it from the bank. The caller knows she can get the money. That's important, Brian. That's important. He steals the money she had lying around the house, yet he knows she has more money available. He rummages through the house, but finds nothing, so he kidnaps her husband."

Because Sammy's voice was muffled, Brian's head popped up from the bed and observed Sammy's head down on the desk. "You're not crying, are you?" he said.

"Almost," Sammy said. He raised his head and sat back in his chair. "Mary won't go to the police, because of what they may find out about her and the money. Now Mary wants our help. We already know about her kidnapping, but she thinks we won't turn her in to the police."

"We will, though. Right, Sammy? We have to tell Detective Phillips what we know."

"Yes, we have to, Brian."

Brian relaxed his head back on the bed. "She said she didn't recognize the voice of the person calling. It was disguised in some way. It must be 'Carl.' His voice always sounded phony to me."

Sammy's cell phone rang. Brian sat up on the bed. Sammy held up his hand to Brian. He opened the phone. "Hello," he said.

Voice: "Could I speak to Sammy?"

Sammy: "This is he."

Voice: I'm Thomas Mason, John's brother. John's wife gave me your number."

Sammy: "Yes, hello."

Thomas: "Emma said that you and a friend are doing work for John. Something about a Rose Marie."

Sammy: "Yes."

Thomas: Pause . . . "Can you tell me what's going on?"

Sammy: "Our work is confidential, at the request of your brother before he died. It is still an ongoing investigation."

Thomas: "I know that. Since he was my brother, I thought I could be of some help to you."

Sammy: "Unless you know some new facts about Rose Marie or your brother, I don't see how you can be of help."

Thomas: "John didn't do anything wrong, you know."

Sammy: "You sound like you have something on your mind."

Thomas: "I always felt that John was carrying a heavy load. You know what I mean?"

Sammy: "And just before he died, he unloaded it to me. Is that what you mean?"

Thomas: "You get my drift exactly."

Sammy: "As I said before, I can't talk about the case. Unless you can tell me more, I must end this conversation."

Thomas: "Thanks for nothing."

Thomas Mason was the first to hang up.

"Who was that?" Brian said, standing and walking away from the bed.

"John Mason's brother, Thomas. He wanted to know about our investigation. You heard what I told him. He may not know about his brother kidnapping Rose Marie, but he suspects something."

"Maybe he was a partner in the kidnapping." Brian said.

"Not according to Mr. Hershey. John went back to Harrisburg on his own. And besides, John didn't need help. Rose Marie went willingly."

The phone rang again.

"Busy day." Sammy said, opening the phone.

Sammy: "Yes?"

Voice: "It's MaryTilson."

Sammy: "Yeah, what's up?"

Mary: "He called again. I told him I have to withdraw the money from the bank tomorrow morning. He wants to meet and make the exchange tomorrow afternoon at 3:00."

Sammy: "Where?"

Mary: "He said he would contact me tomorrow and tell me where to meet him. He said the exchange would be in a safe place. No police are to be contacted, or I would never see my husband again."

Sammy went back in thought to his original theory and walked through it. He made new adjustments. He added his version of what might happen tomorrow. Regardless of the outcome, even if his guesses were wrong, he still knew the players and their possible role in the caper.

Mary: "Hello, are you there?"

Sammy: "I'm here. Do you still want our help?"

Mary: "Yes, but under no circumstances are you to call the police."

Sammy: "I can't promise you that."

Mary: "Then forget it."

She hung up. The call was ended.

"Who was that?" Brian said.

"Mary. Whoever is holding her husband wants the money tomorrow afternoon at 3:00. He didn't say where, just that it would be a safe place."

Brian's face displayed pain. "How are we going to play this?"

"The only option we have is to let Detective Phillips in on the operation," Sammy said with resolution.

"That sounds right," Brian said.

Sammy opened a drawer and pulled out a phonebook. "Mary wants no police, so she wants no part of us. We are not to interfere."

Brian turned away from the bulletin board to see what Sammy was doing. "Does she think we're just going to walk away from this?" he said.

Sammy shook his head. "She should know that, no matter how this plays out, she must be ready to face the police as Rose Marie Maxwell."

"She's the victim," Brian said. "The people in trouble, now that John Mason is dead, are Henry

Hershey and his wife. They're responsible for taking her in, knowing that she was kidnapped."

"If the police believe the rescue spin," Sammy said, "the Hersheys may be seen as heroes for saving her from unsavory, abusive parents."

"What's with the phonebook?" Brian said.

Sammy flipped some pages as he decided who to phone first. "I have some calls to make. The way I see it, 'Carl' is the threat at the moment. Regardless of what Mary wants, we must intervene and reveal 'Carl' for what and who he is."

"And Carl is . . .?" Brian said.

With no proof to back him up, Sammy said, "He's the man we will tangle with tomorrow."

CHAPTER TWENTY-THREE

The sun's rays started the morning as a tourist delight. However, Mary was not delighted to draw the last of her money from the bank. In her three-year marriage to Michael Tilson, she tolerated his irregular earnings as a realtor and his "men-are-all-alike" faults. However, she did love him. That love propelled her to meet the demands of his captor. If her earlier life were to be exposed by the two teen detectives, her marriage to Michael would help her survive the trauma of being discovered.

At the bank, Mary signed the necessary papers to receive such a large withdrawal of $200,000. The bank afforded her the services of a security guard to see her home safely. From home, she awaited the promised phone call.

The call came at precisely 2:30 that afternoon. The disguised voice gave clear directions. She was to come alone, bring the money and her cell phone, and go to the Bird-in-Hand Family Restaurant parking lot. He would be watching. If she wasn't being followed, he would call her with further directions.

Mary thought it strange that the caller directed her to drive from Manheim to Bird-in-Hand. That's where Sammy and Brian lived, the teens who knew the truth about her and wanted to involve the police.

The restaurant's parking lot was full, but Mary found one spot open as someone drove away. A white cloth covered the large, plastic shopping bag beside her. She glanced at other cars, hoping to see someone showing an interest in her. All the cars were empty. An old man and woman were waiting at the restaurant's entrance door. A younger man entered a car bearing New York license plates, but he didn't start the engine. One of two women, probably tourists, was digging through a trashcan for whatever reason.

Within fifteen minutes, the old man and woman were picked up in a cab. The younger man, still in his car, was perusing maps, planning his next Amish experience. The trashcan woman had successfully retrieved her accidentally-dropped pamphlets and with her friend, laughed all the way to their car.

Mary's phone rang.

The voice told her to turn right onto the Old Philadelphia Pike and, at the light, to turn left onto North Ronks Road. She was to keep the phone active and he would direct her as she drove.

Mary kept checking the rearview mirror. He

had to be in one of the cars or the truck behind her, but which one? She hoped her phone battery would hold out for the duration of the trip. Where was she going anyway? She had no idea where she was. Incoming gray clouds were putting a damper on the already scary situation. As time went on, she wished she had the help of the boys. She doubted her decision to reject their help, even if it did include the police.

After ten minutes of twisting and turning around the countryside, she was told to enter the next farm lane, park by the barn, and take the money inside. She checked the mirror. No trucks or cars were visible, but he was out there, somewhere.

Even with the barn door open, the dull sky shed little light inside. She felt a chill and tightened her grip on the money. "Michael, are you here? Michael!" she yelled. She walked deeper into the semidarkness, glancing from side to side. She heard noise in the back, then movement.

A dark figure emerged, coming toward her.

"Give me the money," it said.

"Where's Michael?"

The figure pointed. "He's up in the hayloft, bound and gagged. Put the money on the ground and back up, and I'll release him," the graveled voice said.

Mary did as ordered.

As the figure advanced, the floppy hat, sunglasses, and an obviously fake mustache came into view. After reaching and clutching the bag, the figure ascended the ladder to the hayloft.

Mary waited, allowing time for her husband to be untied and released. She heard her husband's voice express happiness at being freed from bondage. Seconds later, Michael Tilson, wearing his dress suit, punctuated with snips of hay, climbed down the ladder. Mary rushed at her husband. He turned and embraced her as they both collided, savoring the reunion.

"Are you okay?" Mary said, looking into his blue eyes.

"I think so." Michael brushed his hands down over his clothes, pinching and shaking his trousers. He looked over Mary's shoulder and saw two people walking into the barn.

Mary turned and said, "Mom and Dad, what are you doing here?"

Henry Hershey and his wife strained their eyes, peering into the semidarkness of the barn. Henry shrugged and said, "We were told to come here."

Another figure entered the barn. "Hi, I'm Thomas Mason, John Mason's brother."

Mary was overwhelmed and bewildered at the same time with the return of her husband and the unexpected intrusion of the others.

Then, to compound matters, Sammy and Brian walked in.

CHAPTER TWENTY-FOUR

The super sleuths went directly to Mary and Michael. "Hi," Sammy said, extending his right hand to Michael. "Remember us? I'm Sammy Wilson, and this is Brian Helm."

"Sure, you were at the house." They shook hands.

Brian climbed up into the hayloft and disappeared.

Sammy glanced around the barn. "Has anyone seen Carl Rutter?" he said.

Michael motioned up to the hayloft. "He untied me and took the bag of money and ran out the back door."

Sammy smiled and said, "How did you know your kidnapper was using the name Carl Rutter? Only Brian and I knew that."

Michael paused and turned white. "Well, I . . . He told me his name."

"Why would a kidnapper tell his victim his name?"

"I . . . I . . . It wasn't his real name," Michael said.

"How did you know it wasn't his real name?" Sammy said.

"Ah, ah, he told me," Michael said, trying to gain control.

"So the kidnapper told you his name, but then he said it wasn't his real name." Sammy looked up at the hayloft and said loudly, "Does that make sense to you, Detective Phillips?"

Detective Ben Phillips came to the edge of the loft and looked down. "Three police officers and I were hidden out back. No one came out that door." Phillips held up some clothing. "If he had, he would have been without clothes." Hanging from the detective's hand were men's clothing, including a droopy hat, sunglasses, and a fake mustache.

Brian appeared beside Detective Phillips. "Here's the money," he said to those down below, and held up the plastic shopping bag.

Mary finally understood and pushed away from her husband. "You! You! You did this to get my money? Why?"

"I did it for us. Don't you see?" He gestured toward the teens. "These geeks were about to report your whereabouts to the police. You know what that means. The headlines will read, *'Rose Marie has been found.'* Then the money you stole goes back to your parents."

"Which brings us to the blue dog," Sammy said, inching closer to Mary.

"What about my dog?" Mary asked, becoming defensive.

"I wondered why you took the blue dog," Sammy said. "When John Mason came to take you away from your abusive parents, you went back into your house to retrieve a toy dog. Furthermore, to get the dog, you needed to drag a chair over to the window valance, climb on it, and reach for the dog. That blue dog had to be important to you, as important as escaping from your parents, and it wasn't because it was your favorite toy. I never saw the dog in the six childhood pictures of you." Sammy looked up. "Remember, Brian, when I asked you about your favorite toy as a child?"

"Yeah, my dump truck," Brian said, standing dangerously close to the edge of the hayloft.

"I asked you what became of it," Sammy said.

Brian nodded. "And I said it's probably in a cardboard box, battered, with one wheel missing."

Sammy continued. "Yet, Mary, your blue dog is as pretty and new as when your mother added it to her dog collection. The dog was never played with because it was never yours, was it, Mary?"

Mary Tilson/Rose Marie Maxwell saw movement at the open barn door. When three police officers entered from outside, she froze. "No," she finally said, "the blue dog is not mine."

Sammy continued. "Inside that blue dog was your passport to a better life. Inside that dog was a paper containing an offshore bank account number along with a four-digit PIN number. That was all you needed to make the money yours."

Mary's eyes glanced down, her body slumped, and her hands covered her face. She took a deep breath and lowered her hands. "When I was 8 years old, I woke up at 2:00 one morning. I heard voices downstairs. I snuck over to the stairway and looked down. It was Mom and Dad, talking about money, illegal money. Dad had wired it to a bank in the Grand Cayman Islands. Mom wrote the account number and PIN number on a slip of paper, so they would remember the numbers. I watched as she stitched the paper inside the blue dog and replaced it with the other dogs above the window. I didn't know it then, but later I saw it as payback time. So I took the dog when I left."

"That's why you didn't want to go back home," Sammy said. "Your parents soon discovered that you took the blue dog containing their private bank account numbers."

"That was part of it," she said. "The rest is that I don't know my real parents anymore. All I remember is the pain and the rejection and knowing they didn't love me. Why would I want to go back?"

"What did you mean when you said John Mason gave you the money for your nest egg?"

"When John brought me from Harrisburg to his house here in Lancaster County, I told him about the dog and the bank account numbers. He said we should transfer the money from my parents account to my own account before they discovered that the dog was missing and changed the account numbers. So John did it for me. He transferred the money into a different account in my name. He said I had suffered enough and that the money was to be my nest egg, money that would be there when I needed it later in life. I could withdraw the money when I turned 18 years old."

Brian, who wanted to contribute to the conversation, looked down and said, "John probably thought he was doing the right thing at the time."

Sammy continued, "Emma Mason, John's wife, gave me the names of those in the hospital when John Mason died. One name was missing. Your name, Mary, was the only one not included on the list. You were the nurse on duty. I checked it out."

"Yes," Mary said proudly. "I arranged to be there with the man who saved me from my horrible parents. I heard him record the message to you, confessing what he had done. I told Michael what had happened. He said I was not to worry about the kidnapping being exposed. He said he would handle it. I guess he became Carl Rutter, and you saw how he handled it."

"Why did you have the money at home?" Sammy asked.

"I took some money out of the account, in case I was forced to turn over the bank account to my parents. Michael knew about the money." Mary stared at her husband. "I didn't know he wanted it all for himself."

"It was for you, Mary. I did it for you," Michael said, starting toward her.

Mary shoved her husband backward. "You stay away. You knew that if my parents press charges against me, I would go to jail, and then it would be just you and the money."

Sammy glanced up at Detective Phillips. "Have you heard enough?"

"Enough for now. The rest I'll hear at the station," Phillips said, climbing down from the hayloft.

To everyone's surprise, Michael pushed aside Officer Stauffer and made a dash for the barn door. According to his own account, Brian, ever ready to inject himself into any emergency, sprang from the hayloft, launching himself at the fleeing man who once called himself Carl Rutter. Brian landed on Michael's shoulders and knocked him off balance into the arms of Officer Miller. Handcuffs were quickly applied, putting Michael definitely into custody. Later, witnesses would say that Brian accidentally fell from the loft, landing on Michael.

Detective Phillips gave the orders. Officer Stauffer was to take Thomas Mason in his car. Officer Miller was to take Mary and Michael Tilson in his car. Officer Fisher was to take Mr. and Mrs. Hershey in her car. Sammy and Brian went with Detective Phillips.

The extra invited guests had parked their cars behind the farmhouse, out of sight. They had stayed there until Sammy and Brian had walked them to the barn.

When the boys and Phillips exited the barn, heading for Phillips' unmarked car, they saw Michael's black car. Sammy slapped Brian on the back. "There is your infamous black car, Brian— Penn State sticker and all."

Brian shook his head. "Four years of college didn't teach Michael Tilson everything."

"No, some things have to be learned by personal experience," Sammy said.

As the Hersheys were put into a cruiser, Henry was heard saying, "But it was really a rescue, not a kidnapping."

CHAPTER TWENTY-FIVE

"Hi, Amy," Brian said as he captured one of two vacant swivel stools at the U-shaped counter. Sammy glided in and claimed the second stool. The seating arrangement was different at the Bird-in-Hand Family Restaurant. Whereas Brenda's Snack Counter at the farmer's market had high wooden stools, these metal stools were lower, with soft seats and backs.

"I heard you boys had a busy day today," Amy said. "I can't wait to read about it in the paper." Amy Gossert was a counter server, a veteran of 12 years.

"You don't have to wait," Sammy said. "Brian will tell you more than you want to know right now."

Amy made a face and said, "I'll wait and get the unembellished version."

"Yeah, well, the news people may miss the scoop that I stopped the villain from escaping." Brian puffed out his chest and stretched his shoulders back. "Yes, yours truly, at the risk of great bodily harm, pounced on the hardened criminal and hastened his capture."

"What Brian is saying," Sammy said, "is he fell from the hayloft and landed on the man trying to escape from the police."

"Hey, I *leaped* from the hayloft after calculating my weight and the distance to the escapee. My mind and body landed right on target." Brian hugged an imaginary figure. "I clung to the evildoer as the police assisted me in the capture."

"You should be celebrating," Phyllis said, walking over from the gift shop area. Phyllis Gamber was the gift shop supervisor.

"We are celebrating," Brian said. "That's why we're eating here with you and Amy."

"The real reason," Sammy said, "is we were late for supper at home, and my parents are tending the store until eight tonight." He held up a twenty-dollar bill. "My dad gave us money to eat out." He slapped the bill down on the counter.

"This isn't right," Phyllis said, pointing to her left. "You should be eating in the large dining area."

"The entertainment is better here," Brian said. "The only entertainment you get in the dining room is *Happy Birthday* sung by the servers."

Phyllis turned away, doing the two-step. "Well, if you expect Amy and me to sing and dance for you, forget it. I must get back to work anyway."

"Want to see the menu?" Amy said, visualizing herself singing and dancing like in musicals.

Sammy and Brian ordered from the menu and got back to assessing their afternoon adventure.

Brian said, "How did you figure out the meeting place would be in the barn?"

"Remember your conversation with Michael Tilson in the barn? Of course you knew him as Carl Rutter then," Sammy said. "You mentioned about the floorboards making a good hiding place. Well, when he stole the money at home from his wife, where was he going to hide it? He couldn't hide it at or near his house. Mary might find it. I put myself in his place. Where would I hide the money? The answer was the barn. It's a safe place with no one around."

Brian sat back in his seat, winked, and said, "Being a realtor, Mr. Tilson knew the farm would be unoccupied until the estate was settled. Right, Sammy?"

Brian took his stool for a spin. Sammy caught him the third time around, before he slid to the floor.

Never one to admit a weakness, Brian said, "I'm okay. I'm just a little dizzy from hunger." Brian propped his arms on the counter. "See? The counter isn't spinning anymore."

"When you were home today eating your lunch, Mary called me," Sammy said. "She said the caller would be meeting her in a safe place. He certainly felt safe in the barn when he had you. So at noon,

Dad and I went to the barn where you were held captive. The barn floor was made up of wide planks. I looked for a recently disturbed board. I found one with sawdust and a freshly sawed end. Under it was the money in a metal box. I was then confident the barn was going to be the meeting place."

Brian said, "You reported it to Detective Phillips, telling him the whole story. Right, Sammy?"

Sammy nodded. "I gave the box of money we found to Phillips. He and I arranged the surprise party. I phoned and invited the other people of interest. I wanted them to see and understand the conclusion of our investigation. I didn't ask Mrs. Mason to attend. I didn't know how she would react to her husband being a kidnapper."

Brian took a sip of water from the glass in front of him. "I guess Mary Tilson/Rose Marie, the Hersheys, and Michael Tilson will all be facing jail time."

"Most likely," Sammy said. "It depends, though."

Brian spread his napkin on his lap."Depends on what?" he said.

"On how much the judge sees it as a *kidnapping* compared to a *rescue*."

Brian repositioned the napkin and tucked one corner behind his belt. He glanced up at Sammy. "Do you think John Mason had second thoughts later about whether he rescued a girl in distress or rescued a thief in the making?"

"No, because the situation changed from Rose Marie stealing the blue dog to John Mason transferring the money into an account in Rose Marie's name. The girl didn't withdraw the money until she was twenty-three years old. Then her husband stole it from her."

Brian made a face. "This whole case is a mess. I knew it from the beginning."

"John Mason is the one who manipulated the money," Sammy said. "And remember, the money is illegal. The police will confiscate it." Sammy paused and then asked Brian, "Why did you stuff part of your napkin under your belt?"

Brian said proudly, "To keep the napkin from sliding down to the floor." He saw Sammy's quizzical look. "Okay, so I'm short. With my feet on the floor, my lap slopes down. You're 10 inches taller than I am, and you have longer legs. When you sit, your lap is flat. You don't have trouble with sliding napkins." Brian produced a melodramatic sneer. "Some detective you are that you had to ask."

Sammy shook his head. "I've had a busy day," he said.

"I'm ready to eat," Brian said, glancing around for Amy.

"John Mason did wrong by transferring Maxwell's money into a different account in Rose Marie's name," Sammy said. "I believe he regretted it later. That's why he confessed to us. He wanted us to investigate and make a judgment call on our findings."

"Aren't judgments up to God's laws?" Brian said.

"God takes care of *heavenly* judgments. I think John Mason was looking for an *earthly* judgment. He wanted to be remembered as a rescuer rather than a kidnapper."

Brian leaned closer to Sammy. "So what is our verdict?"

Sammy reflected on the last several days. "*My* verdict is that there are good people who make the wrong decisions. It happens when the opportunity of the moment presents itself as a 'better life.' John Mason saw a 'better life' for himself and Rose Marie by taking her from her abusive family. He no longer would have the nightmares and guilt of leaving her behind after he moved away. When the opportunity came for the Hersheys to have the child they always wanted but couldn't have, they made Rose Marie part of their family. They saw it as a 'better life' for themselves and for Rose Marie."

"Which was a bad decision on their part," Brian said.

Sammy nodded and continued. "For Rose Marie, her parents' illegal money offered her an even 'better life.' For Michael, her husband, John Mason's confession exposed his wife. The money would be confiscated. He didn't want that to happen."

"They all had good intentions, but they broke the law," Sammy said. "They made bad choices."

"Yeah, but some people might say they made good choices," Brian said.

Sammy saw the truth in Brian's statement. "Do you know what William Shakespeare said?"

Brian struck a pose and said, "In this case, he would say, 'To be good or not to be good? That is the question.'"

"I was thinking of, 'there is nothing either good or bad, but thinking makes it so.'"

Brian twisted his face as he thought about that and said, "So, Shakespeare is saying that something can be good or bad, depending on how a person thinks about it."

"Right," Sammy said. "During the Second World War, Werner von Braun helped Germany develop and launch the V-2 rockets against London. To the Nazis, he was the 'good guy.' To us, he was the 'bad guy.' After the war, Werner von Braun started building rockets for us instead of Hitler. His work landed us on the moon. To us then, he was the 'good guy.' To the Nazis, he was the 'bad guy.'"

Brian bounced the edge of this hand around on the counter. "It depends on which side of the fence you're on whether the grass is going to be green or brown."

Sammy grinned. "Brian," he said, "I'd like to hear your opinion on this case."

Brian saw Amy approaching with their food. He frowned as he reached for the salt shaker. He couldn't handle intense conversations. He wasn't one to think too deeply about how people's actions affected their lives.

Amy placed the food in front of the aspiring

detectives and said, "You boys   look so serious. What's the problem?"

"Amy, we'd like your opinion," Brian said. "What are your thoughts on this? The story starts with a kidnapped girl and a blue dog . . ."

THE END